Patience

By: Jasmine Johnson

Cover By Laney Fisher & Lance Smith

Book One of The Event Horizon: Virtues

This is a work of fiction. Names, characters, businesses, places, events, locals, and incidents are either the product of the author's imagination or used in a fictitious manner. Any resemblance to actual persons, living or dead, or actual events is purely coincidental.

Acknowledgments

Thank you to everyone who supported me while I wrote this book. Especially my Mom who never got mad at me storyboarding over her all of her whiteboards.

And a special thanks to Kiona and Lili for teaching me the *value* of patience.

Prologue - Michael

I crossed over the flawless white marble to kneel before his throne, "You summoned me, Father?"

His white aura reached me even at this distance. The mere pressure from it made my white wings curl into my back. He is upset. "Yes, Michael. I have received some... *Unfortunate* news."

Unfortunate news? From the reports I had received, Zion was thriving. It cannot be the humans that have upset him, since Zadkiel is tasked with the care of Earth. The only thing left was Lucifer, but he has been mostly silent since the last battle. After a loss that tremendous, he shouldn't have any courage to confront our Father.

I could feel Father's agitation growing, "The Old magics are awakening." I kept my head bent. Looking up would come off as disrespectful. Disrespect would be a grave mistake, even if Father wasn't as agitated as he is right now. But, surely he wasn't talking about The High Virtues. They'd been asleep so long, my brethren had begun to believe they were never real. "I believe your fallen brother has begun searching for the Sins, but hasn't had any success." That is good news. "As for the Virtues, I sent out scouts some time ago, and they believe that the first has been found. I need you to collect it."

"What would you like me to do with it once I have it?" Legends say that the Virtues hold unimaginable power. The kind that could destroy

Zion in a single blow. Perhaps killing it early is our only option.

"To be decided. If it doesn't come willingly, you are allowed to use force. However, I hope the Virtues come to us willingly."

I nodded, completely understanding. *Something* is causing them to awaken. If we want to still be standing when it comes to pass, we will need them on our side by choice. I rose from my kneeling position, "Location?"

"A place called Telluride, Colorado. Zadkiel is ready to direct you. Oh, and Michael," I tuned back to my Father to see a small smile on his face, "The Virtue seems to believe that it is human."

Wonderful.

Chapter One

I'm late. Too late for it to be okay. Maybe Brian will go easy on me if I tell him what happened.

"What the fuck?" I cringed at the anger in my father's voice. There's no way I'm going to be able to make it out the door without being seen. I stepped out of the hall, hurrying to the front door, "Hey!" He slurred, "Why the fuck is my beer warm?"

"The electricity is off," I replied, tying my shoes now that I'm not running out of the house. "I'll call the company today, and see if we can work something out until payday. Water is good warm."

I slipped out the door before he could yell that 'real men don't drink water' or something similar. Seems we both found out about the electricity in unfortunate ways this morning. For me, it was when my phone was dead this morning, and the battery powered wall clock in the hall let me know that I was three hours late for my shift.

I peddled as fast as I could to work. Luckily, there weren't very many cars on the road - everyone else in Telluride must've made it to work on time. I chained my bike to a stand by the front of the store, and darted inside.

Brian - my manager - was waiting near the door when I came in. He was frowning with his arms crossed behind the check out counter. Oh no. "Afternoon, Medusa."

I winced, "I'm so sorry, Brian."

"The store is empty. Wanna tell me what happened?" Okay, so maybe he isn't that upset.

"My electricity got turned off. It was on when I went to bed, but off this morning. So my phone didn't charge and my alarm didn't go off because my phone was dead. I'm so sorry." I'm so fired. I don't know anywhere else that's hiring. How am I supposed to pay the bills?

"You're not fired." My head snapped up in surprise. I was three hours late! He wouldn't be wrong to fire me. "You've been here a long time, Medusa. You're a great employee, and this is the first time you've done anything wrong. We'll call it a warning. Go clock in." He waved me away.

"Thank you! I won't hug you - because I know you don't like them - but just so you know, *I really really want to!*" I darted toward the back room to clock in before he could change his mind. I could hear his quiet laugh as I left.

忍

Four hours later, I was at the counter helping some tourists. Brian ghosted when we'd gotten a sudden rush of them. I didn't mind though. Tourists are one of my favorite parts of the job. I love new people.

"Have a great day!" The happy family of four waved cheerfully as they left.

The customer behind them was an older woman that seemed a bit flustered. I helped her unload the abundance of items in her ams. She should've grabbed a basket. She smiled at me while she struggled with her large floral purse, "Thank you, erm..." She squinted at my name tag. I scanned her items quietly, not offering my name. "Does that say *Medusa?*"

"Yes, it does." I chirped, trying to keep a light tone.

"That is awful! Why would your parents choose an awful name like that?" The smile remained firmly on my face. People often asked that when they learned my name.

"My mother didn't see it that way. She studied Greek Mythology in college, and - personally - didn't view Medusa as a monster. To her she named me after a strong and resilient woman."

The woman scowled, "Well I think it's terrible. Didn't she think the other kids would bully you?"

I hummed, still scanning her items, "Perhaps the problem is with the children that bullied me, and not with my mother. Your total is thirty-three, fifty six."

She begrudgingly handed me two twenties, "You cannot blame kids for that. Kids bully other kids, it's a part of growing up."

My smile dimmed at the ignorance of that comment, but I kept it on my face. Hospitality is the most important part of my job. I handed her the change, "Have a wonderful day!"

She grabbed her bag, but paused before leaving, "You know, it's really a shame." I stayed quiet, waiting to see what was next. Normally, the word 'bullying' was the end of the conversation. "You are such a beautiful girl, but no man is going to marry a monster." She shook her head, leaving the store.

Brian approached me cautiously. I hadn't noticed him come back to the front, but here he was. She must've been the last of the rush. I smiled widely at him, trying to blink back the moisture pooling in my eyes.

"Welcome back." I smiled at him best I could.

"For the record, I would marry you in a heartbeat, but you're a little too patient for me. *That* was bullshit." I nodded in agreement. That woman was more upset with my name than most. "I think it's time for your break. In fact, I think you should take your favorite candy bar as well. No charge." He looked horrified at me almost crying.

I choked out a laugh, but did grab a Hershey's bar as I went. I collapsed into a chair in the break room, and let the tears fall. Today has been a little worse than most. I still hadn't called the electric company; I need to do that before Dad comes up here. I don't think I can handle anything else right now. Deciding to get it over with, I made the call.

Twenty minutes later, I left the break room and went back to the counter. Brian smiled cautiously at me as I came back, as if I was some frightened rabbit.

"I'm okay now. Thank you."

That seemed to relax him a little. He left me at the register, disappearing into the aisles again. The store was quiet for the next few hours; something I'm eternally grateful for. Sometimes I just need a break, and in a tourist town like ours that's almost impossible. Brian left me alone with my thoughts as I worked until about thirty minutes before my shift was about to end.

"Are you alright?" He looked annoyed. He never looks annoyed when I'm working.

He crossed to where I was straightening the candy display and sighed, "As a matter of fact, I am not. Amita just called. She's 'sick' so she won't be here today."

"You don't think she's sick?" Amita had a tendency to catch any illness that came through town, and called in sick a lot, but it doesn't seem like she'd lie about it. Why would anyone lie about being sick when they could tell the truth?

Brian gave me a flat look, "On a Friday? Doubtful. She's probably going out with some of her friends, and decided work wasn't important. I'm sure there will be a bunch of pictures all over all *eight* social media pages she has."

"I can cover her shift." Unlike most people it seems, I actually enjoy my job. Home is stressful and unpredictable whereas work is calm, quiet, and I get to meet new people every day. Who wouldn't want to be here?

"Really?" I nodded, possibly a bit too eager, but Brian didn't notice. Well, he probably didn't care. "Thank you! Thank you! I swear, Medusa, you're an angel or a saint or something equally as pure."

I laughed, "Hardly." I'm certainly no angel or saint. "I'm just a girl who loves my job. When do you head home?"

"One hour." He cheered flatly, waving his hands in the air. I laughed. He's so interesting. "Mac should be here around that time to take over for me."

Oh. That's... Good? It isn't that I don't *like* Mac. He's just, difficult to be around. I could handle a few hours. It's better than being at home.

Brian hung around the front with me for the rest of his shift, and helped me with the few customers that came through. It was oddly peaceful. Brian is great at being company, but not constantly in search of conversation. When Mac got here, Brian all but skipped out the door. He wished me 'good luck!' and left to enjoy the rest of his day.

I worked quietly, hoping to avoid Mac's attention, "Hey, Gorgon." I sighed quietly, but didn't look up. Here we go. Mac was the perfect all American guy with blonde hair and blue eyes that spends too much time in the gym. It's a shame that he has less personality than an insect.

"Hello, Mac. Do you need something?" Probably not. He just likes to use the only word from Greek Mythology he knows. Like when a toddler learns their first word and says it a million times a day.

"Just making sure you're doing your job." So I was right.

Instead of a reply, I ran through my mental list of things that I've done so far. Mac looked annoyed at my neutral tone, but didn't get the chance to further attempt to agitate me as the door chimed, signaling a new customer. Mac grew pale as he looked past me to the newcomer. Odd.

Oh, that's why. The man was beautiful. He was well over six feet tall with golden blonde hair that fell over his broad shoulders. He must be a model that came for his vacation or something. Poor Mac probably felt threatened as 'The Hottest Man in Telluride' - his words not mine - with this man here. Is this what you'd call karma?

"Welcome! How can I help you today?" I chirped, going to meet him at the edge of the counter.

His blue eyes focused on me, momentarily unnerving me. There was no light in his eyes. They were a shocking shade of blue, but they held no humanity or compassion. It... It was terrifying.

"Medusa Sinclair?" His voice was so melodic. It was almost soothing, but with those eyes... How could eyes be so dead?

"That's my name! How can I help?" Eyes or not, I can still be nice.

He nodded, "My name is Michael. I need to speak with you." His eyes flicked to Mac - who was shamelessly eavesdropping beside one of the shelves. He glared at Mac, *"Alone."*

That... Didn't sound safe. Before I could ask Mac to stay, he shrugged and wandered to the back. Michael seemed pleased. I resisted the urge to shrink behind the counter. Instead, I pressed my palms into the countertop, and faced him with a smile.

"I have placed a barrier around us, so he cannot listen from the second aisle that he is currently hiding in." Honestly, I wouldn't be surprised to find Mac actually hiding behind the second aisle, but how would he know if he is? What 'barrier' is he talking about? We're just in the store. "Now that he cannot hear, I am the Archangel Michael, and have been sent by my father Yhwh - human's commonly address him as God. I have been sent to begin your training."

Training? God? I don't know if we have an asylum nearby, but someone is definitely looking for this guy. Maybe he's done some type of substance? I think rich people do that when they're bored, right? I smiled, trying to appear as harmless as possible, "Okay. Do you need me to call someone for you?"

He scowled at me. Oh no. "Do not patronize me. You know you are not human, Medusa. Not fully, at least. We are not quite sure what you are, yet." His head cocked to the side as his scowl deepened. "The human is coming back. We will have to finish this later. What time do you leave here?" Before I could answer, he continued speaking, "I am bringing down the barrier now. *Speak wisely.* I am not here for execution, but I will if I have to." *What?* He can't seriously be talking about killing people!

Mac came around the end of the front aisle, and Michael's eyes seemed to lose all traces of the slight warmth they held. I turned my focus back to Michael, "I leave at eight."

He nodded with a small smile that seemed a little too forced. As if he was just pretending to be an easygoing person, "I will see you tonight then. Eight is late in the day, I will bring food." Then he was gone.

Once he was gone, Mac marched up to me with a deep scowl, "We have strict rules with personal affairs while on the clock, Gorgon. If you want to flirt with your boyfriend, do it on your own time." He barked.

"He isn't my boyfriend." I denied, keeping my voice calm. There's no point in getting upset about his antics. He could turn me in for an 'outburst' and get me in trouble with Brian or the owners.

"I find that hard to believe," He scoffed, "I saw the way he smiled at you. If he isn't buying anything, keep him out of here."

"Okay." He was taken aback by my complacent reply. It was like *not* arguing with him made him angrier. Boys are so strange. Mac stomped away from me, fuming silently.

With Mac angry at whatever I did, I was left alone with my thoughts, and they centered solely on Michael. Who was he? Maybe it was some odd church recruitment thing? He was talking about God - no wait, he called him something else. Yhwh? I think. What a strange spiel. Maybe it was just a joke being played on me by someone... Maybe it was Emilie? She spends time with the models and celebrities, perhaps she talked one of them into it. It's been years since they played a prank on me. Maybe reliving their high school days? Then again, I don't even know if Emilie or the rest of that group are even in town right now...

With that strange man keeping my mind occupied, my shift was over in the blink of an eye. I helped Mac close up the shop, before hopping on my bike and heading for home. The lights were on when I got home, running up the electricity bill I just handled. I rolled my shoulders, trying to loosen the stress knots that were forming. The front door opened as I walked up, revealing Michael.

"Welcome home, Medusa." He stepped back, letting me in my own home. My father sat on the couch with a beer in his hand, and several more scattered around his recliner. He didn't seem bothered with the stranger in our home. "I brought you your usual from *Steamie's*." How does he know I love *Steamie's*? "They even gave you extra fries. It is all very... Unhealthy."

What? *Steamie's* is one of the healthiest places to get a burger and fries in town... I guess they do know my order by now so maybe he didn't have to read the menu. "Th... Thank you." I chewed on my bottom lip, looking through the paper sack. I led the way to the dining room.

Michael joined me at the table with his hands folded in front of himself. "I brought your father some of the '*Steamie Dogs*' as well, but he has already finished them." He pronounced '*Steamie Dogs*' slowly as if they were unfamiliar. That does explain why dad was so complacent. Still, he should know to not answer the door to any random person that appears. Michael shifted, "I have reinstated the barrier. Your father cannot hear us." I bit into my burger, waving for him to continue. "I am going to explain while you eat. You may ask any questions as I explain.

"As I said before, I am the Archangel Michael, and I have been sent here by Yhwh to begin your training. You are one of Heaven's Seven Almighty Virtues." Virtues?

"Virtues? What are those?" He said there's seven as well. He didn't seem bothered about me interrupting him - that's good.

"Virtues are the best traits a person can have, and the actual Virtues are the perfect examples of their respective Virtue. The Seven Almighty Virtues are Patience, Chastity, Kindness, Diligence, Humility, Temperance, and Generosity. You are the first Virtue we have located, but do not focus on that. We have my brethren working on finding the others. For now, you and I are going to work on your magic, and preparing you for what is ahead." Well that sounds ominous. Michael didn't stop to elaborate though. "So, what magic do you have?"

"Hmm?" He expected me to know? "I have no idea. I don't even know what Virtue I am. Am I supposed to have some type of magic?" I cleaned up my mess, before sitting back at the table.

Michael stayed quiet while I wiped the small mess off the table, but continued to think quietly well after I sat down. I waited for him to finish. The only other sound in the house was the game on the television. It was oddly peaceful. It's a beautiful evening today. Maybe Michael and I can talk outside for a while.

"You truly do not know which Virtue you are?" I turned back to Michael, shrugging at him. I had no idea which one I could be. Honestly, I don't think I could qualify as the perfect example of anything. "Medusa," Michael smirked at me. His blue eyes seemed to take on some warmth, too. He almost looked normal... Well, normal for an outrageously beautiful person at least. "You don't know which Virtue you are?"

"Nope," I shrugged, "Sorry, but I truly have no idea. Is there a test I should do? Are you sure it's me?"

He laughed a short quiet laugh, "Medusa Sinclair, we have been sitting at this table in *silence* for forty-five minutes. You are the Virtue of Patience. You did not speak up once."

"It looked like you were thinking. I didn't want to disturb you." I was just being polite. What if he was thinking of something important?

Michael shook his head, "Do you want to know what I was thinking of?" I shrugged. It was his business really. He doesn't have to tell me. "I was counting. Two thousand, seven hundred and thirty seconds of silence. Silence that you didn't interrupt. *I* had to break it."

Oh. "Well, I guess you're the angel, so you'd know." He was the most experienced, right? "So, what's next?"

Chapter Two

"Are you not cold?" Michael asked standing beside me. It wasn't that chilly yet. Over the next couple weeks the temperature would go down significantly, but tonight wasn't so bad. "I was under the impression that humans struggle under sixty degrees. It is around forty-five now."

"Nope! I think it feels great." There was a breeze tonight. I could almost taste the crisp bite in the wind. I led him over to the babbling brook that ran through our yard. It was still water this early in the year. I took a seat beside the rocks, patting the grass for Michael to sit beside me.

He reluctantly sat down, sighing quietly. "As far as Earth goes, Telluride is not so bad."

"It really is beautiful. I'm so grateful to live here." I dipped my hand in the cool water. I could feel Michael's eyes on me, but he didn't speak. Is he waiting for me again? "When you said training, what did you mean?"

"One thousand, two hundred and thirty seconds." He *was* counting! Who can count that high without losing their place? "When I say training, I mean your magic. We need to figure out what your magic is, then begin to develop it." Well, he makes it sound easy. Maybe he has a plan. "So, have you ever... Frozen anything?"

"Not that I've noticed." I do live in a ski town that snows a lot. "Is that what your magic does? Do you have ice powers?" That could be cool.

"Yes." He held out his hand. Little flurries swirled in his hand, taking an odd shape. A moment later the flurries spun away, leaving a pristine ice sculpture of a pegasus behind. It was stunning. "Here." He handed it to me.

"Th-Thank you." There were so many details. I could see each individual feather on its wings. It's beautiful. Moments later, the entire thing was a puddle in my hand.

Michael sighed, "You're too warm for ice." Oh, I've disappointed him. I apologized, folding my hands in my lap. "Do not apologize." He snapped. Now I've made him angry? Well this isn't going well. "You are a legendary Virtue of Heaven. We will discover what your magic is. It will just take time."

"I'm sorry that I'm not much help with this, Michael." I shifted. "Is there anything I can do to help?"

"Yes. Stand up." I followed Michael off the ground. What ever we need to do, I'm ready. "Are you familiar with Krav Maga?"

"Nope! What is it?"

"Then let us begin."

忍

I whimpered, wrapping my arms around myself. The hot water prickled on my skin. Maybe if I got it hot enough, I wouldn't be able to feel how badly my body hurt anymore. Michael and I tried Krav Maga, but there was no sign of my powers, so he insisted on trying something else called Northan Shaolin. I'm not a fan of either to be honest. None of my magic appeared either. I was still just a regular human. Well, a regular human in a lot of pain.

I don't know where Michael is now. Last I saw, he was talking with my father about whatever was on the television. I can't stay in the shower too long though. Water bills aren't cheap, after all. I shut off the water, and dreaded picking up the towel that was waiting for me. Another whimper escaped as I wrapped the towel around me. I can't believe I have to work tomorrow. Maybe I have some pain pills laying around... Probably not. Dad eats them like they're Skittles, so I typically don't buy them.

With the towel wrapped loosely around me, I made my way out of the bathroom to my bedroom. "Welcome back." I jumped at the sound of Michael's voice. Why is he in my bed?! I didn't think a queen bed could look so small. Michael seemed to dwarf it with minimal effort.

"What are you doing in here?" I clutched the towel tighter against my body.

"Your father instructed me to wait in here for you." Michael sat up, patting the small spot on the bedside him. "Come sit. There are things we need to discuss."

"I'm not dressed! There's nothing under this towel, Michael. Can you step out so I can get dressed, please?" It seemed to dawn on him, and he moved from the room. I moved as fast as I could - which wasn't as fast as I normally could because I kept having to pause. I braced myself on the closet door, sliding to the ground. I'll get dressed in a few minutes. Maybe I can... Maybe I can just close my eyes for a minute.

"Medusa." I blinked up at Michael. His figure wavered in front of me. Was he holding something? "Stand up. Come on." He pulled me to my feet. When did I sit down? I don't know if my groans of pain made it out of my mouth, but if they did, they didn't deter Michael at all. I could feel my legs trembling underneath me, threatening to make me collapse again. "Stand. Just for a moment. Put your arms out." I listened to him, I think. I can't tell if I'm still moving. I feel like I'm wobbling.

Michael slipped something over my arms, before moving in front of me to do something else. "Alright. You don't have to stand up anymore. I will catch you." I sagged, falling into Michael's arms. He carried me to my bed, and tucked me in. "We will talk in the morning. Sleep."

Chapter Three

"How are you so weak?" Michael watched me move around the room at a snail's pace. He didn't sleep in here, but came in at the sound of my alarm this morning. Apparently, he had dressed me in a night shirt last night, and put me to bed - at least that's what he told me. Considering all he's been doing this morning is taunting me, I'm almost positive he made it up. "We didn't do that much training last night. It is barely a scratch on the surface on the training we need to accomplish."

Oh *fun*. That sounds enticing.

"I have to go to work before we do anything else. Ah!" I froze with my shirt still on my head. Anytime I stretched my arms too far, my muscles seemed to seize for a moment. I'll be okay in a second. I think.

Suddenly, my shirt was pulled down. Michael glared at me, "Arms, or I will do it myself." That sounds painful. With Michael's help, we got my shirt on.

"Thank you, Michael." I glanced into the mirror. My hair was in an anti-gravity mood today it seemed. "Is there any chance you know how to fix hair?"

Michael pursed his lips, "It looks fine." So, no then. I'll just have to brush it myself then. "Give me that. You look ridiculous." Michael took the brush from me. A little too forcefully if you ask me, but it felt nice to have someone brush my hair. Honestly, I can't remember the last time someone else brushed my hair. It must've been Mom. "There."

"Thank you, Michael." I laughed, "I sound like a broken record, don't I?" Ooh, laughing was a bad idea. I'll have to remember that. Michael didn't laugh or comment, he simply opened my bedroom door waving for me to go out first. Maybe one day I'll get him to laugh, or smile. Smile seems a bit easier to accomplish.

"Hey, would you smile if we learned what my magic was?" I smiled up at him.

He scowled back, "Unlikely. *However,* your magic appearing would make my life easier." Close enough.

"Medusa Sigyn Sinclair!" I flinched at the sound of my full name. Dad was angry, but why? I checked the fridge last night. We have plenty of beer, and food he doesn't have to cook. He was standing in the living room with his arms crossed when we made it to him. "What is this?!" He gestured to the neatly folded blankets on the couch. How did those get there?

"That was me, Elias." Michael spoke up, "When I found them, they were crumpled on the couch, so I was not sure of where to put them when I got up. Where do I move them to?"

"No no, Michael." Dad smiled warmly at him. I guess *Steamie Dogs* make friendships. "This is not your doing. You're a guest here! You don't have to sleep on this frumpy old couch! From now on, you take Medusa's bed, and Medusa will sleep on the couch." What? "Because that is *how you treat a guest.*"

"Oh. Right." I nodded, "You take my bed from now on, Michael, and feel free to use my room while I'm gone." Dad was right. I should've made Michael take my bed last night instead of making him sleep on the couch. I grabbed my bike, feeling my back already aching in thought of this ride. At least Whittle Corner isn't that far.

"Medusa." Michael followed me out, holding something in his hands. "This way. You are in no condition to ride that today." He waved for me to follow him to the car parked in front of the house. When did that get here? I know it wasn't parked there yesterday. I would've noticed.

"Michael it's okay. I'll take myself. You can work on whatever it is that you work on." I don't need to be any more of a bother to him.

Michael turned, blue eyes blazing, "*You* are what I work on. Get in." I set my bike back where it goes, and moved as quickly as I could to the car. "Here." He dropped a banana in my lap. We don't have bananas in the house. Where did he get this? "Eat that. I will get you something more suitable when we get into town."

"That isn't necessary! I'll be okay. Thank you for the banana." Michael didn't reply. Once I was done with the - extremely delicious - banana, I glanced over at him again. Maybe I should say something. Is he counting again? What if he's just thinking about the day ahead? Then interrupting him would be rude. So I should stay quiet... Right? I'll just stay quiet. Just in case.

"Welcome to Whittle Corner, we have just what you- Medusa!" Brian just about vaulted over the counter. "Just for that, I'm buying lunch!"

"Just for what?" All I had done was walk in the front door, with someone extra no less.

"You're twenty minutes early! Have I ever told you how much I love you?" I am? I guess that makes sense. Cars are a lot faster than bikes. "What do you want for lunch? *Steamie's*?"

"No!" Michael snapped, startling both of us. "No more burgers. I am going to get you breakfast - a *real nutritious breakfast* - that she will eat whether she is working or not. *You* will find something for lunch that is not a greasy burger or fried anything. Do I make myself clear?"

"Umm, *Steamie's* isn't fried or greasy... That's the poi-" I caught his eye, shaking my head. Michael is determined to believe that all burgers are greasy it seems. Brian nodded back at me, avoiding Michael's glare. "Yes, sir!" Brian nodded rapidly. He looked like one of those sport bobble heads my dad collects. "I'll find something healthy. Do you want anything... Um?"

"My name is Michael. All I want is for you to assist me in keeping Medusa alive, by not feeding her *garbage*." Then he was gone.

I threw away my banana peel, and went to clock in. Brian was shaking his head as I passed, "Your boyfriend is intense. He's also obviously never had *Steamie's*. Hey, are you okay? You're walking weird. Actually, don't answer that. Never mind."

"He's not my boyfriend, and I'm okay. Thank you for asking." I moved to the back with measured steps. In case any customers came in - and partially out of fear of Michael - Brian stayed in the storefront. Luckily since it was a cold day I got away with a long sleeved shirt, so there wouldn't be even more questions.

Michael hadn't meant to hurt me. He just severely overestimated how much strength and fighting knowledge I had. Honestly, I think Michael was under the impression that - what did he call him? - Yhwh, I think, had sent him to recruit a warrior. Too bad all he found was me. I'll just have to try harder.

"Medusa, there you are." Michael was holding a brown paper sack and a foam to-go cup. "I have gotten you a green tea smoothie, and a salmon and sweet potato breakfast burrito with spinach, eggs, and cottage cheese as well." Oh.

"What an... Intriguing combination." I took the bag from him, trying to hide my grimace. Maybe it doesn't taste as bad as it sounds. "Thank you, Michael."

Brian scowled, "That sounds awful, but you do you. Michael, are you going to stay here during her shift?" When Michael turned back to him, he raised his hands as if Michael was a police officer. "Not that I mind! Go ahead and hang out. Just, ah, try not to scare the customers. Please." Brian moved to the opposite end of the store. We probably won't see him again for a while.

I pulled the burrito out of the bag, feeling the dread growing in a pit on my stomach. This was the biggest burrito I've ever seen. "Um, Michael, I won't be able finish this. It's too big." I don't think I've ever had this much food as one meal before.

"Do your best. You need the strength."

"If you say so." Oh. *Oh. That's so bad.* I blinked away the moisture in my eyes. Does he really expect me to eat this? I actually like all of these separately, but *together?* There's so much cottage cheese. Green tea doesn't help! It makes it worse! I made it halfway through the burrito and tea before giving up. "I'm so sorry, Michael. I can't. Please don't ever give me another."

Michael made a noise, "Is it not pleasant? I believe they are all edible."

"Edible doesn't really mean they taste that good together." I gave the bag with the burrito back to the angel. "Thank you, though. I appreciate the effort, and I am no longer hungry." I don't think I'll ever be hungry again. Just the thought of food is making me nauseous. I don't know if I'll be able to hold it down at all.

"I see." He glared at the bag, "I will return later. If that man brings back one of those *godforsaken grease carriers* you are to not eat any of them." I shivered. The temperature seemed to drop to freezing in mere seconds.

I gulped, "Okay!" He left, taking the chill with him. I don't think I'll be able to eat another burger again. Well… That's not true. I just won't eat them around him.

I grabbed the to-do list Brian left behind. Since he's disappeared, I'll go ahead and finish them. His parent's always give him an incredibly long list for the mornings and it makes his anxiety act up. He doesn't need that stress on top of everything he actually does.

I grabbed the cart of things that needed to be re-shelved, and began putting them away. The higher shelves hurt more to stretch to, but I managed. It was quite some time before the bell on the front door chimed, signaling Michael's return.

I moved to the end of the aisle to greet him, "Did you finish your… Oh." It wasn't Michael. It was actually a group of people I had gone to school with.

"What? You aren't going to greet us?" Yvonne taunted, smirking at me. Yvonne was someone I had grown up with. She was raised in Telluride along with her brother Lysander, and their friends Emilie, Gideon, and Fenix. They're also the sole reason I didn't enjoy high school as much as I thought I would. Well, that isn't completely true. Lysander didn't bother me much. He didn't seem to be in the group either... He must be overseas for a modeling gig.

Still, I straightened my shoulders and smiled, "Hello! Welcome to Whittle Corner - we have just what you need, *whittle* or big! How may I assist you today?"

Yvonne pouted, "What? That's all we get?" She laughed. She seems to be in a good mood today. I wonder what has her in such high spirits.

"You seem to be in a good mood today, Yvonne. Enjoying this weather?" It did seem to be turning into a beautiful day. I haven't actually seen this entire group together in quite some time. There seems to be someone else with them now though. Surely, they didn't just replace Lysander.

"Of course I am. After all, it's a beautiful day to show Mr. Blue our magnificent little town." She gestured to the new member of her group. Mr. Blue? That sounds familiar...

"It is a cute town, Yvonne." Mr. Blue smiled at her. He seems kind. "However, you can call me Allan. You know that." Yvonne blushed. Maybe it's the accent? A lot of people go nuts over the British accents.

I guess that means they don't need help then. I moved back to the cart full of miscellaneous things I need to put back. Why did so many people put candy back? I've never seen this much in the basket before. "Medusa! Where did you go?" I jumped, moving back to where Yvonne can see me. "Don't disappear like that. I didn't bring him to see this shitty store. I brought him to see you."

"Me?" Why would she bring someone to meet me? I don't think Whittle Corner is bad. Sure, it's nothing like the big grocery stores, but it's cute and homey. It has character.

"Mhmmm! Allan, this is Medusa Sinclair resident outcast of Telluride. You see, Allan needs to do research for his new roll coming up. Who better teach him how to be a reject from society than you?"

Oh. I kept my smile up, "That is very nice of you to do for him. What is the role for?" That explains why the name sounds familiar. He's an actor. I don't know what he's been in, but I don't really watch movies... Or tv... Or anything really.

"It's a secret." Emilie snapped, "He can't tell you that!"

"She wouldn't know that, Emilie." Yvonne rolled her eyes. "Her world doesn't pass the town line." I wish that was still true. Heaven seems to come with a lot of stress. "It's simple, Medusa. All you need to do is talk to Allan for a minute. Allan, trust me. She is the best person for this. Her mother died when she was little, her father has been a miserable drunk for as long as we can remember, he doesn't work so she's forced to work countless hours here to support them in a house they can hardly afford anymore. School was miserable for her. Her clothes were always too small or from decades before. Kids bullied her mercilessly," Kids specifically being everyone standing in front of me right now, but I suppose that isn't worth mentioning. "Not even her father feels love for her. She's a true outcast of society. It's perfect!"

Allan looked taken aback, "Oh. You've had a terrible life." It isn't that bad, but Yvonne wouldn't know what my life has been like. Sympathy and pity swarmed in Allan's eyes as he took a step toward me. "I'm sure it can't be easy having it thrown in your face like that. Yvonne she's not a character in some movie. She's a person." Allan moved to me after giving Yvonne a sharp look. "I'm sorry about he-" As he reached out to me, a large hand grabbed his wrist.

Michael towered over him, glaring fiercely, "Who are *you* and what makes you believe you are allowed to touch *my Medusa?*" His Medusa? Since when do I belong to him? I suppose he sees me as his, because he's my mentor, but does he realize how that sounds to other people?

"Wait, who are you?" Emilie moved to look up at Michael. How odd. I haven't seen her look at anyone like that since she had that crush on Mac in middle school. "And why on Earth is a guy like you, with someone like Medusa?"

Michael's glare focused on the woman in front of him. He should like Emilie and Yvonne. They're both gorgeous tall women with wafer thin figures. I believe both have been recruited for modeling. They're much more angelic looking than I am. "Are you the ones responsible for the tears gathering in Medusa's eyes?"

Was it that obvious? I can't cry at work two days in a row. That's horribly unprofessional. Maybe I can force them back by blinking? Nope. I wiped my cheeks. All I had done was make them more obvious, because now they're running down my face. Man, this has been a week.

Michael grew angrier, making me shiver. The temperature beside us seemed to be dropping again. Is this because of his ice magic? I hope that isn't my magic. I don't think I can handle being that cold all the time. I'd have to wear my coat everywhere, or move to Texas. He released Allan's wrist, "Medusa, are you alright?"

What? "Oh, I'm alright! Everything she said was true. Slightly painful, but true. It's alright. I'm alright. You can calm down. It's okay."

Michael turned his frown on me, "Do not lie to me, Medusa Sigyn Sinclair." My eyes darted to the ground. I'd rather him be mad at anyone else that isn't me. He seems to be much more grumpy than he was when he left this morning.

"*Sigyn?*" Emilie grimaced, "I didn't think your name could get worse. What does that even mean?"

"She's another woman from mythology that my mother thought was a symbol of strength." I explained. My names don't make me uncomfortable or ashamed. Sigyn and Medusa have incredibly interesting stories, and my mother had a few journals where she spoke about how much she admired the two.

Emilie didn't seem to agree. She scoffed, "Your mother named you after fairytale villains."

"I don't remember her asking for your opinion." Michael snapped. "Do the five of you plan on buying anything?"

"No," Yvonne crossed her arms, glaring up at Michael. It's much easier for her to accomplish considering she's several inches taller than me and much closer to Michael's face. "You are being extremely rude! Do you know who we are?"

"Insolent little brats with too much pride is what you are." That... Seems harsh. This is just who Yvonne is. She doesn't really think about people like me. "If you are not here to shop, I suggest you leave."

"Or what?" Fenix - speaking up for the first time - stepped forward, "You do realize you're threatening two girls right?"

"I am not threatening two girls. I am offering the five of you a chance to leave before I forcefully remove you." Michael didn't seem bothered at all. Personally, I think Felix can be a little intimidating. He's tall and muscular, and seems *very* angry. He's still shorter than Michael, which probably explains why Michael isn't fazed. Well, that and the whole celestial being thing. "And I can guarantee that you will not win this, *boy*."

Wait. He's not planning to hurt them in the store, is he? *'I am not here for an execution, but I will if I have to.'* That's what he said yesterday.

"Michael." His blue eyes had an odd golden sheen to them. I don't think that's a good sign. I moved to stand beside him, placing an arm on his - alarmingly thick - bicep. He was freezing. "Please don't."

Michael sighed angrily, stepping back. My sigh of relief didn't go unnoticed by him, though. His eyes snapped back to the group, *"Get out."*

Four of them scurried out, but Allan remained. He ignored Michael, and focused on me. "I apologize for her words, Medusa. I was under the impression that we were going on a tour of Telluride, not coming to patronize you. I sincerely apologize." With a final nod to Michael, he followed the rest of the group out of the store.

"Thank you for shopping with us!" Brian greeted as he came back in. When did he leave? I didn't hear him leave. He was carrying bags of food though. "Was that Allan Blue?"

"Yes. When did…"

"What did you bring? It doesn't say *Steamie's*, but that doesn't mean there aren't burgers in there."

"No, but the utter fear you put in me earlier made sure of that. I got food from *Sérénite.*" Oh, wow. *Sérénite* was a nicer French restaurant in town. I've never actually been, honestly. "I got you a lemon peppered salmon salad with green artichokes. I don't know if you like those, but it sounds healthy."

"Thank you." I took the salad from him, and the offered plasticware. Oh, he got a honey mustard dressing too. How… Appetizing.

Michael peered over my shoulder at the salad, "It has many healthy elements. Eat all of it."

"Well, don't eat more than you can handle," Brian interjected, "It is a big salad." I smiled at him. I didn't think he'd care about my eating habits.

Michael rolled his eyes, "It is not that big." It was one of the biggest salad's I have ever seen. Maybe it doesn't look big, because he's some type of frost giant. I wonder what he'd think of something really tiny. Like a kitten.

Ignoring Michael completely, I turned back to my outrageously kind boss, "I'll eat as much as I can before I get back to work. Thank you, again."

"No problem. Anything for my best employee." As long as it doesn't upset Michael. He didn't say it, but with the way his eyes kept nervously shifting to the ice giant, it's a little obvious. Maybe I should talk to Michael about not purposefully scaring Brian. Not that he'd actually listen to me.

忍

"Alright," Michael turned to face me. He had patiently waited while I changed out of my work uniform into what could be considered training clothes. They were just sweats, but I think they'll work. Maybe I should've picked up some type of elbow pads on the way home. "Are you ready to begin?"

"Yup!" I had taken some pain medicine before we left the store, and couldn't really feel the bruises from last night, so I should be ready for whatever he's planned. "What are we trying today?"

"We are trying Aikido and - if that doesn't work - we will try Muay Thai." I don't know what either of those are, but Michael seemed optimistic about them. Maybe they'll work. Then I'll have real life magic like *Matilda*!

忍

"Oomph!" I landed on my back, again. I find it very hard to believe that people do this is for fun. "I don't think I like Muay Thai. Are you sure it isn't a torture method?"

"I am positive." Michael stood over me, he looked perfectly fine. We've been out here for two hours. He looks like he's just been standing here this whole time. I wish that is what he'd been doing. I'd be in a lot less pain that way. "Get up. I want to teach you the Tae Chiang. Surely one of these will get your magic energy flowing."

"Can I please go shower and lay down?" I don't know how often he does full contact sports - is martial arts a sport? - but I never do them, and I'm exhausted. I don't think I can feel my legs.

Michael sighed, pulling me to my feet, "Yes. I will be in shortly." Sounds good to me. Maybe he'll stay out until I'm actually dressed this time.

My father didn't say anything as I made my way through the living room. He was too invested in some football rerun. I wonder if he knows we have more channels.

"Medusa!" I jumped, nearly falling back down the stairs. "Grab me a beer while you're in there." Sighing internally, I moved back down the stairs to the fridge. He glanced up at me to take his drink. "Dear god," He did a double take. I don't think I've ever seen him actually focus on me like this. "You look awful. Go shower before Michael sees you like that!"

Why does it matter if Michael sees me like this? He's the one that kept knocking me over. I'm off tomorrow. We should spend the day looking for a training area inside. The ground is just going to get colder as we get deeper into winter. At this rate, I'll end up with frostbite before November.

I stopped by my room to grab clothes before heading to the bathroom. Just in case Michael comes inside before I'm out. I'm already a bother to him, the least I can do is actually get myself ready for bed. He wasn't too happy when he told me about last night.

I kept the shower temperature lower than I would normally have it. My skin is already so cold, too much heat seems like a terrible idea. At least I'm not in too much pain. Maybe the pain medicine helped past and future pains. That's nice.

Michael wasn't in my room when I came back. Odd. I wonder if he's still outside. Maybe he enjoys sitting outside in the cold, or he's too angry to look at me right now. It's probably the latter. I don't know why his methods aren't working, but my magic is staying dormant. If I even have any. I don't think I'm the type to have magic, honestly. Michael won't hear it though. He's convinced I have some somewhere in my subconscious.

Wait. What if I dive into my subconscious? Oh, where's that book? I moved to the bookshelf that was embedded into the wall. Once I was old enough to read, I had gone to the basement to see if she had any books I could read. It was where I had found her journals, and massive books on mythologies from around the world. I had also found several books on meditation and the human subconscious. Here it is!

I settled in the middle of my bed, folding my legs underneath me. Okay, I'm in a quiet place - well the quietest place I have access to. Now I just need to take deep breaths, and... Imagine myself sinking deeper into the bed. I can do that.

I closed my eyes - the book said I could choose something in the room to focus on, but that will just make me think. I need to not think. Just breathe, and sink. In and out. Deeper into the bed. In and out. Deeper into wool comforter. Now picture my perfect day...

I'm in a nice sundress with little plus and multiplication signs all over it. A room full of third graders sits in front of me, eyes bright with fascination at what they could learn today. It would have exercise balls instead of those awful plastic chairs.

"Medusa!" I jumped, completely losing focus. Michael stood in my doorway with a large smile on his face. I made him smile! "Do that again!"

"What? I was just meditating. I thought it would help with my magic, but I don't think it did anything." I certainly didn't feel any different.

"Is there a window open in here?"

"No?" All of my windows are closed. It's thirty degrees outside.

"Then why is there a breeze?" What? Wind blew through my hair, sending it flying. How is he doing that? I thought he just made ice? It wasn't a cool breeze though. It was pretty warm, and - oddly enough - quite comforting. "Medusa, you're the one doing that." He bent over to grab something from the floor. It was the book that was sitting in front of me five seconds ago. Did I blow it off the bed? "Is this what you were using? Show me where you were."

He climbed onto the bed, mimicking my position across from me. I took the book from him and went back to the chapter I was reading. Michael read it over a few times, before reading through the rest of the chapter. I sat quietly, letting him read through it. He better not be counting. Letting someone read in silence is a courtesy thing, not a patience thing.

"I never considered meditation. Do you have enough energy to try this tonight, or would you rather wait till morning?"

I felt much better, actually. It was like I'd drank one of those Monster drinks everyone had in high school. "I'm good to go for now!"

"Excellent. How do we do this?" He left the book open in front of us, so he could peer at the directions without having to change his position. "Meditation is not something I do often, or ever, actually. This will be a first."

"Well, I've got some great news! Unlike your teachings, I don't plan on causing you any physical or mental pain." I straightened my posture, but relaxed the rest of my body. Michael followed my movements. "You're supposed to be relaxed, Michael. Just let go."

"Relaxation leaves you weak. I need to be prepared for any and all attacks."

I tilted my head at him, "Attacks? Are you expecting someone to try and hurt us?"

"There is always an opportunity for someone to hurt others. Humans hurt each other all the time without reason. Even your father could randomly decide to come in here and attempt to end your life. All it would take is a slight shift in the way his brain functions."

I laughed. Michael's frown got impossibly deeper, but I couldn't help it. It would take more than a *slight* shift for my father to deem me more important than the television. "Can you just relax for a moment with me please? I want to see if I can actually *do* something with these powers you insist I have."

"I insist, because I knew they were there, and guess what; I was correct. If we get attacked durning this 'relaxation' of yours, I will never let you forget it." I believe that. Michael shifted uneasily, glancing at the windows on either side of my bed. The angel took a deep breath, and released it letting it take all of the taught tension in his body with it. "What next?"

"Close your eyes-"

"The book says that I can focus on an object in the room."

"Well, I know you and you can't. If your eyes are open, you will be focused on what could happen or what is happening. Wether it's a bird or an assassin. Close your eyes." Looking like an angry grizzly - growl included -, Michael complied. "Release the tension. Stop growling, that's how I know you aren't relaxed."

"Stop *giggling* and I will be more relaxed."

I bit my lip, and actually listened to my own directions. How am I supposed to teach Michael how to do this, if I can't even show him I can do it? "Okay, now focus on your breathing. After every measured breath, I want you to picture yourself sinking deeper into the bed."

"Alright." He breathed.

We sat there quietly. I could hear every breath he took. He wasn't breathing loudly though. In fact, it was almost soothing. "Okay, now picture your perfect day."

"No. I want you to picture this room." My room? I could just open my eyes for that. "Trust me. Picture the room, feel the air currents. There are at least two, as we are both breathing. Focus on those."

"Umm, okay." I kept my eyes closed and pictured my room. In my head I could see Michael sitting across from me with both of us breathing with our eyes closed. This is weird.

"Now I want you to move the air that you are focusing on. Just try to move it slightly."

I don't really know *how* to move air, but I told him I'd try my best. Maybe I can just grab it and pull? I don't think it's working. Okay, so what if I inhale, and imagine breathing in all of the air. A hand landed on my calf, nearly sending me off the bed. Michael inhaled deeply, trying to catch his breath. What happened?

"Are you okay?"

"Yes," He coughed, "You did fantastic. You took the air right out of my lungs. Literally." Oh!

"I did it?" Is he serious? He wouldn't really play a joke on me, would he?

"You did it."

"Yay! Oomph," I rolled off the bed. Maybe throwing my arms up without actually sitting in a stable position wasn't the best idea. Michael looked over the edge of the bed, raising a brow at me. "My bad."

He shook his head, "You are such a human."

"But I did it!" I held up a hand for a high five. Michael simply grabbed my hand and pulled me back up to the bed. "I wanted a high five, but thank you."

"I don't know what that is, but I will pass." Of course he would. That will be my next goal. I got him to smile when I made my powers work. Now all

I need is a laugh and a high five. Shouldn't be too hard, right?

"Well, we should probably go to bed now. I'll move to the couch, so you can rest." Michael caught my hand before I could get off the bed.

"That is unnecessary. You can stay here." I shook my head. He heard my father this morning. "I will stay in here as well, so your father does not get upset. Don't worry. Just go to sleep."

Michael moved to lay in the bed, patting the space beside him. I guess he's serious. I shifted, looking down at the bed. "I usually sleep on that side..."

"Oh." He shuffled to the other side, and pat my usual spot. "Now get in, and sleep."

"Is this a normal thing in Heaven?" I asked, climbing into the bed once I'd turned out the lights. Michael wasn't under the covers, but seemed comfortable enough. "Sharing a bed with someone else, I mean."

"We don't have beds in Zion - which is the correct name of Heaven. I only experience exhaustion in the human realm." Really? What is it like to never need or want sleep? I can't imagine that. I think everything should take the time to recharge. "So, I don't actually sleep, but I have been needing to take some time to recharge."

"Oh. Well, goodnight Michael."

"Goodnight, Medusa."

Chapter Four

I flipped the pancake, humming quietly. Honestly, I don't know why I'm in such high spirits this morning. The air just felt... More crisp this morning. We must have a cold front coming in.

Speaking of cold fronts, Michael smoothly came into the kitchen. "Your father is not in his normal spot. Did he leave the house?"

"It's eight in the morning," I laughed, "He's still asleep, I'm sure. Do you like pancakes?"

"I don't eat." He peered over my shoulder anyway, to get a look at the pancake in the pan. "This does not look healthy, Medusa. I will go get you something else."

"No! No, thank you." I don't ever want a repeat of breakfast yesterday. "I've already made these. I don't want to waste food." He frowned down at me, then at the plate stacked with pancakes. "I'll eat some fruit on the side, okay?"

"That sounds a little better. I recommend avocado."

"That's not happening. I'll have an apple." I turned back to the - now burnt - pancake on the stove, and moved it to a different plate. Michael seemed appeased enough to move to the barstool, and stayed silent.

It's so strange. Normally I don't like days off. They make me stay home and be bored, but today was so peaceful. I wish I could stay in this moment forever. I wasn't alone, so I'm not lonely, but Michael didn't need me to do anything or fill the silence. The tv is off, so I can hear the birds outside. It's just so peaceful.

I slid a plate of pancakes in front of Michael along with the butter and syrup. "Just in case you want to try them. You don't have to eat them." He nodded, going back to looking out the window. Well, they're there if he wants any. I put the rest in the microwave so dad could have some if he wanted any. He usually likes pancakes. "So," I chirped, taking a seat beside Michael. "What are we doing today? More meditating?"

"In a way, yes. There is a park nearby. We are going to go there, and see if you can connect with your element there." He looked me over, "You will need to change. I don't think penguins are appropriate."

"No," I laughed. I'd had these penguin pajamas for years. They were faded, and torn in more than one place. They were still comfortable, though. "I'll change into something more appropriate." If I was going to be playing with wind, skirts and dresses are a no. Ugh, I don't really like pants.

After washing off both of our plates - Michael had eventually ate his - I headed upstairs to change. Thankfully, Michael didn't move to follow. I slipped into a comfy sweater and some jeans as quickly as I could, and tied my hair up in a ponytail. The last thing I want is to get hair in my face. It would probably kill the 'magical' aspect of all this.

I could hear Michael and my father talking in the kitchen as I slipped my boots on. Dad seemed to be in a chipper mood this morning. Must be the pancakes. Michael looked up as I entered the kitchen, and gave me a strained smile. I think it was meant to come off as easygoing, but he just looked uncomfortable.

"Medusa!" I jumped at my father's booming voice, "Michael let it slip that you two are *closer* than I originally thought. That's wonderful news! He's a good guy this one. I can tell."

He let it slip? Michael didn't seem like he'd accidentally do anything, let alone tell a secret that didn't exist. Michael moved to me, pressing a kiss into my temple. Has he been possessed? Can angels get possessed? "I may have let it slip that we shared the bed last night. Sorry, love, I know you wanted to tell him in your own way."

Oh.

He must've mentioned it casually not realizing how my father would take that. Someone should really make a human handbook for angels. At least Dad is happy about it. Most fathers wouldn't really approve of their daughter keeping a secret like that from them.

"Sorry I didn't tell you sooner, Dad. I wasn't sure how to approach the subject." I don't like lying to him, but something tells me he wouldn't react to magic as well as this. Less of two evils, right? "Are you ready to go, Michael?"

"Yes. Enjoy your breakfast, Elias." Dad smiled at us as we left before focusing back on the fridge. I'll probably need to go grocery shopping soon.

"That was an accident." Michael grumbled once we were both in the car. "I did not think he would take sharing a bed as a courtship."

I laughed, "I think everyone would take it that way. That's what it would mean if you were human, at least." I like this car. It's so cozy. The backseat was mainly for show, but could hold a handbag if needed. It's definitely a lot warmer than my bike on these Autumn mornings.

"Really?" Michael glanced over to see me nod. He shifted uncomfortably, tightening his hands on the steering wheel. I wonder when he learned how to drive. Does Heaven - sorry, Zion - have a driving school? Maybe it's a school on humanity that gets updates every two years or something. Though they seem to be lacking knowledge on common behaviors and meanings. "Well, it is a good cover for why I am in your life so much. You are not 'dating' another human are you?"

"Nope. I've never really had time." Back when I did have time, no one was ever interested in me. When there are always girls like Yvonne around, I'm the last thing anyone is ever thinking about.

"Good. We don't need any meddlesome humans butting in where they aren't wanted. They'll just hinder your process." He pulled into the park parking lot, and peered out the window. "There, by the big tree. That is where we will go."

Oh, I love that tree. It was toward the middle of the park, and easily the biggest tree around. The weekday morning saved us from having to battle a crowd to sit underneath it, too. Michael sat next to me, mimicking my crossed legs again.

"Now, don't pull the air this time. There are some humans around that we don't want to gain the attention of." Michael instructed, keeping his voice low. No one was really near us, but I guess he was just being cautious. "For now just close your eyes and try to feel the air around you and me."

Okay. I can do that. A true meditative state might not be possible for me right now with all of the sounds around us, but I can do what I did yesterday... Right? I pictured Michael and I sitting side by side in the cool shade with the wind rustling the leaves above us. I wonder if I could make a leaf fall... Maybe if I push it a little. Michael told me not to *pull* the air; he said nothing about *pushing* it.

"Medusa?" I jumped, completely losing focus. May stood in front of me, with her uniform in her hand. Her rose gold bob was tousled, but still pretty. She tried to get me to dye my hair with her, but I didn't have the funds to do something that unnecessary. Plus, I don't mind my blonde. "How long have you two been sitting here?" She laughed, bending down to brush a pile of leaves from the top of my head. "You're both covered in leaves! Who's the man? I didn't know you had a brother."

"Oh, I don't have a brother. This is Michael." She was right about one thing though. We were completely covered in leaves. I stood up to shake mine off before brushing them out of Michael's hair.

Michael frowned at me after finally opening his eyes, "You are pulling my hair out of it's coil."

"You're covered in leaves!" I continued brushing the leaves from his hair. He looked like some kind of forest nymph. Maybe a forest giant? Do they have those?

"Well aren't you two adorable." May cooed, "I can't believe you didn't tell me you were seeing someone."

"What?" I snatched my hand away from Michael's hair. I could already feel the blood rushing to my cheeks. "We... We're not... Michael isn't..."

"Well, of course I am. Are you suddenly ashamed of me, love?" I turned to him, feeling my cheeks turning pink. I didn't realize we were telling *everyone* that we were together. News travels fast in a small town, though, so everyone would know pretty soon anyway, I suppose.

"Well," May laughed, "You two are cute. I'll leave you to get back to your couples mediating." She gave me a hug before continuing on her way.

Michael huffed, placing his hands on his hips, "This is turning out to be much more useful than I had originally thought. Humans are so gullible." Coming from an angel that's a little concerning... He turned to me. I shrunk under his glare. What did I do to make him so mad all of the sudden? "I told you to *feel* the air. I specifically told you not to push the air since there are humans - your friend May, for example - around. Humans do not need to witness actual magic; they're greedy enough."

Oh. Yeah, I should've known he'd be mad about that. "I'm sorry, Michael. I just got excited."

His scowl deepened, "Well don't. There is nothing exciting about war."

War? When did war come into this? He doesn't really expect me to *fight* someone, does he? He's mentioned fighting and danger a couple times before, but I thought that was his paranoia. "Michael!" I called, chasing him. I don't know when he started walking away, but he had gotten pretty far. He paused when he realized I wasn't catching up very fast. "What did you mean? Is there a war coming?"

"That doesn't matter right now. What matters is you getting control of your powers. You don't need to concern yourself with the details, I am handling them." I pursed my lips, but didn't reply. It's not like I'm in any immediate danger, right? Michael is here to protect me. If he doesn't think I need to know the details just yet then I should trust his judgement. He is much older than me, and has seen more than I could possibly imagine.

"Medusa?" I looked up to see the guy from the other day jogging toward us. What was his name again? Ellen? No, Allan? I think. I won't say his name out loud just in case. Michael said something under his breath that I'm almost positive was a very bad word in a different language. Can angels curse? I smiled as Allan reached us, "It is so good to see you again. I wanted to apologize once more for the actions of Yvonne the other day. It was horribly unacceptable, and I feel so terrible that anyone would talk to another person in that manner."

"Oh it's alright. I've known that group since kindergarten. They've always thought it was crazy that I didn't have as much as they did. The whole school did, really." Yvonne isn't in the minority here. I am. Always have been.

Allan didn't look convinced, "That doesn't make it okay. Maybe I can buy you dinner or something? Are you free tonight?"

"*No,* she is not." Michael responded for me. I couldn't see him since he was standing behind me, but his shadow stretched in front of us, making his presence even more pronounced.

Allan seemed to shrink into himself as he looked up at Michael, "I didn't mean it like that. I was just trying to be nice. You made it very clear that you two are together the other day." The other day? That was before Michael had mentioned anything about this lie. Allan focused back on me,

"I don't mean any harm to your relationship. I just hoped there was a way I could apologize for that ordeal."

"Don't worry about it." I shook my head. I don't think I've ever met a stranger that was so kind before. "Just the fact that you cared enough to apologize makes me really happy. I hope you enjoy your stay in Telluride."

He beamed at me, "Thank you! I already think I love it here. If I didn't love living in New York so much I would definitely move here." He waved goodbye, and continued on his way through the park.

I've never been to New York, but I don't think it could beat Telluride. I've never traveled though, so there's that. Maybe if I ever travel I'll lose some of my bias.

"Medusa." I snapped back into focus. Michael was standing several feet in front me, looking back at me with his arms crossed. Oh. I guess it's time to go. "I figured you'd be hungry. Would you like to continue working instead?"

"Nope! Food sounds great. Do I get to pick what I eat?"

He shrugged, "Not really. We are not going to one of the eating establishments that are filled with grease. We are going to the base of operations in this district." There's a base of operations for angels in Telluride?

"Oh that sounds fun!" I jogged to keep up with him as he crossed the park. How does he get so far so fast? "How close is it?"

He made a noise, but didn't answer. What does that mean? We made it back to the car without Michael giving me any further information. That's okay though. It's all part of the journey. Right? We got into the car...

And drove right back to my house. This is the base of operations?

"This is my house."

"Very good. We have to leave the vehicle here. Follow me, we want to stay away from your father's eyes as well." I followed him out of the car, and jogged to reach him again. I'm going to need stilts to keep up with him.

We made our way toward the side of the house where there weren't any windows from the living room. Michael turned to me, fixing me with a glare, "Do *not* scream." Why would I...

I slapped my hands over my mouth to stop any of the noises that were on their way out. Gigantic snow white wings unfurled from his back. They were almost as wide as the side of the house. Michael rolled his eyes at me, "Come here. Still no screaming, and *do not* pet me."

I stepped into his open arms, and shivered. He's like a block of ice. "Medusa, wrap your arms around me, and hold on tight." I really should've worn a jacket. I did as instructed, and wrapped my arms tightly around the glacier. Michael's wings wrapped around us casting a blinding light. I buried my face into his chest to try and block most of it out. I think I finally understand the term 'blinding white light' I thought it was an exaggeration.

By the time Michael let me go, I was a shivering mess. I *really* should've grabbed a jacket. Michael frowned down at me, "Why are you so pale?"

"I...I'm...F-f-fre-eezing." Does he not realize how cold he is? Are all angels cold or is it just because of his ice magic?

"Really? I thought it was much warmer here than Telluride."

"I wasn't talking about the weather. Oh, never mind." I turned away from him to get a grasp on our surroundings. There were pine trees *everywhere,* and nothing else. Just trees, and grass everywhere. Surely he didn't bring me to the middle of the woods. How would that be any different than just walking half a mile from where I live?

"Michael... Where are we?" What if he leaves me here? He wouldn't do that... Right? What have I gotten myself into? This doesn't seem like a base of operations to me.

"I believe this is called Sapphire Falls in North Carolina. The waterfall is that way, but it's a tourist attraction. The base is further that way, but not close enough to be in danger from you. I want you to get into touch with your magic here." He pointed to a nearby tree that couldn't be anywhere less than twenty feet tall. "Blow that tree over."

"Um..."

"Do it, Medusa." He stepped away, and crossed his arms.

I guess I don't have much of a choice. I'll just have to try my best.

I focused on the tree in front of me, and took a deep breath. All I have to do is meditate and push the wind, right? I can do that. I faced the tree, and closed my eyes. Even breaths, picture the scene around me, and feel the wind move with me. I could see everything - all the way to Michael's folded arms. The breeze ruffling the leaves on the trees became a mere extension of me, allowing me to curb it any way I want.

Okay. I can do this. I pushed the breeze toward the tree Michael pointed out to me, and heard the wind smash into the tree trunk.

"Did I do it?!" Oh. The tree stood tall, and completely untouched. Not even a branch had fallen.

Michael growled behind me, "Nothing happened! I said knock it over!"

"I tried!" Michael's glare got worse at my reply.

"*Try harder*. We don't have time for these ridiculous baby steps! Do it again, and do it right." I don't know what happened between here and the park, but I don't like it. He's scary when he's angry.

"Okay." I moved closer to the tree, and closed my eyes again. Okay. This is simple. All I have to do is push harder. I can do that. I can do anything I set my mind to! At least I hope so.

The breeze came back to me, along with a few other scattered winds from nearby. Maybe with their help I'll be able to knock the tree over. Then Michael won't be so mad at me. I gathered all of the wind I could muster, and directed it at the tree. By the time I released it, I was short of breath. I tried to focus on the tree to see if it had fallen, but it swayed in front of my vision. Is it falling?

"Medusa!"

Chapter Five

I groaned, rubbing my eyes. How did I get to my bed? I thought we were in the woods. Had he tricked me with some kind of illusion? I didn't think angels could do that.

"Oh good. You're awake." Michael sat beside me on the bed. He didn't seem very happy with me.

"I take it I didn't knock the tree down?"

"No. You fainted and slowed your heartbeat down so much I thought it was going to stop completely." He sighed, pinching the bridge of his nose. "You're too weak."

"I'm-"

"I will return later. There are things I need to discuss with my father. It seems we need to rethink our plan of action. You are not a defender." I sagged into myself as he made his way out of the room. I'd failed him. Michael paused in the doorway, "You have work in an hour. Take your bike."

忍

"Medusa! So glad you're here." Brian greeted with a wide smile. He peered around me, "Are you alone today?"

"Yup! I don't know if we'll see Michael for a while, if I'm honest." He was really disappointed in me this morning. I wouldn't be surprised if he decided to abandon me completely and just go find the next Virtue. Maybe they'll be better than me.

"Oh," Brian awkwardly hesitated, "I'm sorry. Not that he isn't here because that dude is scary as shit, but you seem upset so I'm sorry about that." I laughed. Michael can be pretty terrifying. "Tell you what, I have to go help my Mom with something at home, but when I get back I'll bring you lunch. Sound good?"

"That sounds great actually. I got so busy disappointing Michael that I forgot to pack mine."

"I've got it covered!" He grabbed his phone off the counter, and made his way to the door. He paused when he reached me, putting a hand on my shoulder, "You're an amazing person, Medusa. I've known you for years and have never been disappointed in you. Sure that Michael guy is big and muscly, but that doesn't mean he's a good guy. You could do much better, in my opinion. Please don't start crying."

"Sorry." I blubbered, trying to blink the tears away. That was really nice of him to say. He patted my shoulder once more, promised to have lunch, and disappeared out the door. I think I scared him. He isn't a big fan of emotions.

It wasn't long before the door chimed, signaling a new customer. I straightened to see an older couple waling into the store. The greying woman turned to the man with a wide smile, "Look at this little store! It's so cozy, and adorable!"

"Welcome to Whittle Corner! We have just what you need, *whittle* or big! Is there anything I can assist you with today?"

The couple came over to me with the woman still smiling away. What a happy person. "Oh what a cute little pun! We're just passing through on our way to Albuquerque. I saw pictures of Telluride on that picture app on my phone and have been dreaming of coming here ever since."

"Oh! Well I'm glad you finally made it! I've never been anywhere but Telluride, but why go anywhere when I already live in one of the most beautiful cities in the world?" I wish all my customers were like her. I would love to have such happy people in here all the time.

"Oh you are just so cute! What is your name so I can let your boss know how wonderful you are?"

I smiled, showing her my name tag, "Thank you! My name is Medusa."

Her smile slipped from her face, as her husband frowned, "Medusa? Like the monster?"

"That is one take on it, yes."

"One take?" Her husband interjected, "Is there another take? She turns men into stone."

Some women don't like men, so they would think it's a good story. I can't say that though. Instead I just smiled, "Well now it can be like the nice woman at Whittle Corner."

"We're just going to look around." Off they went. I returned back to restocking the toiletry aisle while they moved around the store. Less than ten minutes later they left the store without buying anything. I guess my name upset them.

A few more guests made their way through the store, but only talked to me when they had to. Which is fine, and normal. I'd rather them ignore me than be mean to me. Sometime later, a girl around my age rushed into the store. I couldn't get the welcome phrase out before she was several aisles deep into the store. I refocused on the destroyed candy shelf until she made her way to the counter.

She carefully sat all of her items on the counter. Yvonne would hate this girl. She seems so effortlessly gorgeous. Her long black hair was falling over her shoulders. She ran her hand through her hair, making it look like an official hairstylist fixed it. Her grey eyes focused on mine, prompting me to actually speak.

"Hi! Did you find everything okay?" I smiled at her, trying to cover up how long I was staring at her.

"Yeah, thank you." Was her husky reply. I didn't realize a husky voice was an actual thing, but she definitely has one. Her head tilted, "Is your name really Medusa?" *Oh.* "I don't mean any offense. I'm just curious."

I tried to bring my smile back up, and laugh it off, "Yeah. I like my name though. It's unique."

The woman actually scoffed at me, "My name is Karma, so I feel your pain."

Karma? That's such a pretty name! I told her so, too. She basically rolled her eyes at me. Is she always this positive? "I'm being serious! I like it!"

She blinked at me. I don't think she was expecting me to be serious. "Oh. Well thank you. Sorry, I'm a little too used to people immediately mocking it." I know how that feels. Customers do that everyday I'm at work. She ruffled her hair again, showing off her massive biceps. Does she benchpress trucks? "For the record, I think Medusa is pretty badass."

A surprised laugh escaped my lips. That's... A strong word. It's nice though! "Thank you! I'm not feeling much like one lately." Michael's disappointed face flashed in front of my face. Maybe I can try knocking down a tree again after work... My life has gotten so weird lately.

"Yeah, me either. Maybe I just need a different teacher." A different teacher? That's an idea... Who would even teach me? Another angel doesn't seem like they would be much better.

I patted her hand that was resting on the counter. It had a grandma feel to it, but it's all I could think to do. She looked really down. "I don't know what kind of teacher you have, but trust me, he can't be worse than mine." I froze, remembering how I let Michael down. "I don't mean to be rude. He's helping me a lot, but he's so mean some times. I don't understand how he can be so grumpy all of the time. It's crazy. I don't think I've ever been angry for more than an hour at most." How can you hang on to anger for so long? Michael seems to always be some form of angry when I'm around. Maybe it's just me...

"So I'm not the only one with a stoic, infuriating man that I have to spend time with?"

"Absolutely not! Do you want your receipt?" She declined, smiling at me. She has a really pretty smile. Is it weird that I want to tell her everything like we've been friends for years? "I'm actually known for being patient, really *really patient,* but it's like God put him on this Earth just to get rid of all my patience. He's like a general. All. The. Time." I groaned, handing her bag over the counter. Maybe I'll get a short break from him and recharge. "Hey, how long are you in town?" I like having her around.

She gnawed on her bottom lip as she thought. Maybe I shouldn't have asked and just let her go. I didn't mean to make her uncomfortable. "I actually don't know. We're staying in a cabin a few miles outside of town, so about an hour, I guess?"

"Well do you want to meet up sometime next week? I'm off Tuesday. We can do lunch and get away from our overbearing men?" Oh god, Medusa. Stop talking. "Sorry if I seem a little over excite-"

Karma laughed, cutting me off, "That sounds great. How about one o'clock on Tuesday?" I couldn't help the excited smile that crossed my face. I think I just made a really good friend.

"That sounds great! We can go to *Steamie's*. It's the best place in town. They serve burgers, by the way. Are you a vegetarian? They have a veggie burger too." She doesn't really look like one. I think you need a lot of protein to keep up with a physique like that, but what do I know? I can barely lift a bag of marshmallows. "Sorry, I keep forgetting you're new in town. I feel like I've known you forever."

The door chimed getting our attention. Michael! He actually came back! Oh. I just made plans for *Steamie's*...

"Medusa!" I jumped at his gruff tone. I guess he's still angry. "There you are." He stalked over, but stopped to scowl down at Karma. "Who are you?"

Oh no. He probably thought she was like Yvonne. "Michael, stop. Karma, you should probably leave before he starts talking." I joked, hoping she'd take the advice seriously. I don't want Michael to end up ruining my new friendship.

Karma took my advice and grabbed her bag. As she went to pass Michael, he grabbed her forearm. What is he doing?! The look Karma gave him was deadly, "Can I *help* you?" I could feel the venom in her words as she glared back at Michael without flinching. He was several inches taller than her, how is she not frightened? She must be a superhero.

I could feel the temperature dropping around us, signaling Michael getting upset. This is going downhill fast. I moved around the counter to get to Michael. "Ow!" Karma yelled, "Get your hand off of me!"

"Michael!" Taking a breath, I gathered some of the air around me and pushed the full weight of my body at his arm with a small wind boost. Not enough for Karma to notice, hopefully, but enough to successfully get his hand to let her go. Once she was free I turned to glare at him. She didn't flinch in front of him so maybe I don't have to either. "What is the *matter* with you?"

"Medusa move." Michael commanded, expecting me to listen. Maybe I would've yesterday, but not today.

"No! You can't do that!" I turned to Karma, "Go, it's okay. I've got him." She didn't seem sure, but listened anyway. Once she was gone, I turned back to Michael. "You *can't* harass the customers! This is my job!"

Michael rolled his eyes at me, "Medusa, there is something wrong with that girl. I'm going after her."

"Too late. Her car just left the parking lot. See?" I pointed to a random car that drove past the window. I don't know if that's really her car, but Michael seemed to buy the lie.

He cursed in that language of his again, watching the car drive off. Hopefully he can't remember license plates. "What did she say to you?"

"Nothing. It was just small talk. It's part of the job." I moved back around the counter. I hope she's okay. "You didn't *hurt* her, did you?"

Michael's frown deepened, "You are not asking the questions here. What did that girl say to you? Did she mention the Virtues?"

"What? No! She's just a nice person who was being nice to me! Do you know the last time someone was nice to me?"

He scoffed, "Yesterday. That boy in the park."

"*No.*" Moisture was gathering in my eyes, adding to my frustration. I don't think I've ever been this worked up. "Not nice to me because they feel bad. Even May is nice to me because she pities me in some way. Not Karma, though. She was just genuinely having a pleasant conversation with me, and you ruined it! She'll probably never talk to me again."

"*Good*. I'm serious, Medusa. That girl was not of this world. Her magic aura was outrageous. I've only seen so much fury in one other being..."

"Maybe she wouldn't have been so mad if you hadn't grabbed her."

Michael's blue eyes flashed a bright gold, "You aren't listening! Stop being so human! That girl has a magic signature that I have only seen in my greatest enemy. That is *not* a good thing. Stay away from her. I'll need to let my father know about her existence." What would Yhwh do to her?

"Wait, Michael..."

"Lunch has arrived!" Brian announced coming through the door with *Steamie's* bags and milkshakes. He deflated exponentially at the sight of Michael. "Hey... Man... What's up?"

"Are those burgers?"

"Get out." Michael turned to me in shock. I straightened my spine. "I'm going to eat that burger, and you can't stop me."

His eyes narrowed, "I can stop him from giving you them."

"Hurt my friends again, and I'm done. I don't care what happens. I won't work with you any longer if I can't trust you. I mean it, Michael. You went too far." Michael stared at me in silence for an eternity, before leaving the store.

I released the breath I was holding, sagging into the counter. "Holy moly... I didn't think I was going to win that."

"Holy moly?!" Brian sat the bags on the counter. "You won't get fired for saying holy shit. That was a holy shit moment! Oh, you don't curse. Well I do! *Holy shit!*" I laughed, "You did so good! Look at you being a strong and confident woman! Thank you, for not letting him murder me. Here, you can have both fries." He handed me the bags after taking his burger out, "Go take your lunch. I got things up here, you *badass*." That's twice now. I think I like being a badass.

I settled into the break room with my lunch. My hands were still shaking from standing up to Michael. I didn't think I'd be able to do that. Next time I decide to be like Karma I should remember that she's a lot stronger than me, and could probably handle much more than I could even hope to. Yeah, I need to find a different way to be strong. Karma's way is a little too aggressive for me.

This burger is amazing. I love *Steamie's*.

"Hey, badass." Brian poked his head in the room. Is it time to go back already? "Where do we keep the powder-less gloves?"

"In pharmacy by the ankle braces. Bottom shelf."

"Thank you. Here." He tossed a chocolate bar at me. I should probably tell him that not all women will be happy to have candy thrown at them when they're upset, but then he'd stop giving me free candy. Plus what kind of girl doesn't like free candy? "Oh," He poked his head back into the room, "That's because you were shaking and I was concerned, not because I think throwing chocolate at women makes them happy."

"It *does* make us happy. Just for the record."

He laughed, giving me a thumbs up before going back to whatever he was doing. I finished my food and my free candy bar, and checked the time. I still had a few minutes. I should probably learn to eat a little slower. Ha! That'll never happen. I love food too much.

When my break was over, I met Brian back at the front. He smiled when I walked in, "Feeling better. Thank you for everything." He waved me off. I forgot he doesn't like sappy moments. "Sorry."

"You're alright. I'll be restocking the shelves and pretending I don't understand any of the customers. Those people that were looking for gloves?" I nodded, "They needed powder-less gloves to go *skiing!*"

I frowned, tilting my head. "If they're going skiing... They would need wool or the leather gloves on aisle four."

"I know! That woman yelled at me, and told me to get you. She thought you were my manager! All because I didn't know she meant skiing gloves instead of the blue ones in pharmacy! You are *not* my manager." He pointed at me. "I'm the manager. Dammit."

I laughed, "I know, and you're a great manager."

"Damn right I am. Here." He handed me another random candy bar from the candy shelf. "And just so you know, I'm keeping track of how many candy bars I give you. That way I don't confuse myself with paperwork, so don't lecture me." I wasn't going to lecture. Maybe. Possibly. Okay, I was, but I'm not the manager.

"Oh look! A car pulled into the parking lot." He disappeared like a cartoon character. There was even a cloud of smoke in his body shape. "Hello! Welcome to Whittle Corner - we have everything you need, *whittle* or big! Is there anything I can help you with?"

The new customers ignored me, and continued past me. Brian would like those people. The next group of people were a family with a little four year old dressed in the cutest ice princess costume I have ever seen. She was carrying a little snowman in her arms, too. How adorable! I bowed to her as she moved passed.

"Mommy! She thinks I'm a real princess!" She cheered, skipping behind her parents. "You can be a royal knight in my kingdom, lady!"

"Thank you, your majesty." She scream-shrieked in excitement, jumping in place. Her parents just laughed, and went back to looking for whatever they came for. I moved back to the counter, but couldn't get the smile to go away. I love kids.

Oh. There goes the smile. Michael was back. He came to rest his arms on the counter, "I have spoken to my father about that woman." I pointedly ignored him. Why would I want an update on how he's ruining an innocent person's life? "Are you ignoring me? How old are you?" I glared. Well, I think I did. I don't glare very often nor do I like to. "*Medusa.*"

"Michael," I snarked back, "Please continue telling me about how you ruined my new friend's life for absolutely no reason other than some hunch you had." Ugh. I turned back to him, laying my hands flat on the counter. "I meant what I said, Michael. If she gets hurt because of you or Yhwh, I will not help you any more. I mean it." I'll just forget I have magic and go back to being boring and not stressed.

He rolled his eyes, "She won't be hurt. Just investigated until we figure out what exactly she is and why she shares the same signature of my worst enemy."

"That's twice you've said that. Aren't you an angel? Can angels have enemies? I feel like that's against the Ten Commandments."

"It's not." He frowned at me. Not a mad frown, just a sort of confused one. "You should learn those, as an agent of Heaven."

I squinted, scratching my head. Oh I was probably ruining my ponytail. "I don't really *want* to learn the Ten Commandments. I'm not all that into religion, honestly."

"You're... Yo- Just forget it. I'm allowed to have enemies, and he is worthy of being called my enemy. Believe me. He's a terrible creature. A terrible horrible *obnoxious* vile-"

"I get it, but I don't forgive you. There's something I want you to do in order for me to want to help you." Michael sighed, ruffling his hair. He waved in a 'Let's get this over with' way. "Do you see that little girl in the blue dress?"

"Yes?" He frowned, staring at the child.

"No no. Don't stare so obviously. That's creepy. Every time she walks past that display fountain, she tries to freeze it with her ice powers. I-"

"That child has ice magic?"

"No. Stop interrupting, and whisper." He leaned forward, mocking my whisper pose. Wasn't appreciated, but at least he was being quiet. "Next time she goes to freeze the fountain, I want you to freeze it."

"Why?" The exasperation was clear in his voice.

"Because it'll make her day. Prove to me you can make someone *happy* for no other reason than for them to be happy." I sat up to smile at the girl's parents, "Did you find everything okay?"

"Yes, thank you!" The mother smiled at me. I checked them out while keeping an eye on Michael from the corner of my eye.

While I was helping her parents, the little princess went back to the fountain. Her face when it froze was a priceless show of pure enjoyment. "Mommy! Daddy! Look! Look!" When her parents looked over, the fountain was water once more. They just smiled and told her that it was pretty. When they looked away and she turned back to it, it was perfectly frozen again. On their way back out, she waved to me, "Goodbye, Lady Knight!"

"Goodbye, Ice Princess." I beamed, waving her out. When they were gone, I turned my smile to

Michael. "Did you see how happy she was? You did that."

"I risked her parents seeing that, but whatever. Are you done being mad at me?"

"A little, *but* no more hurting my friends. What did you tell your dad about Karma?" Why does he think she's abnormal in some way, anyway? She seemed perfectly normal to me. Then again, he did say something about her having a magic signature, so maybe it's some form of magic I don't have.

"That is none of your business. She won't be harmed." That... Didn't sound like the whole sentence, but I'll let it go for now. He did make that kid happy today. That's good enough for now. "When do you leave here?"

"Four hours. Are you staying the whole time? You make Brian nervous." Hopefully he didn't hear me. I was right, but he wouldn't like that. Something about masculinity, I suppose.

Michael rolled his eyes, "I ha-"

"Sir Michael." A tall golden haired boy, probably only a few years younger than me, walked in coming straight to Michael. He actually looked a lot like the angel, other than being much shorter.

Michael nodded at him, "Adakiel, what brings you here?"

"Father sent me. He needs to speak with you urgently. He sent me to watch over the girl." Do I really need someone to watch over me? I'm just going to be working.

Michael glanced at me, then frowned at his... Brother? He called Yhwh father, so surely they're related. "I will return as soon as I can. Do not let her out of your sight." Where would I go? Does he really think I'd just run off somewhere during my shift?

"Yes, sir." Adakiel nodded, moving to stand behind the counter.

"Oh no." I stopped him at the little swinging door, "You aren't allowed back here. You don't work here." Michael rolled his eyes, but I held up a hand. "I could get *fired*."

"Fine." He huffed. He grabbed a stool from behind the counter - without actually getting behind the counter. Being tall must be so nice. He sat the stool toward the back of the counter where his new friend could watch me without freaking out my customers. Adakiel took the seat with his eyes firmly focused on me. This should be fun...

"So, how are you liking Telluride, Adakiel?" The angel just sat there silently. I guess he isn't much of a talker. That's okay I'm good at being silent. Really good at it. Michael gets annoyed with how silent I am. So I can tota- Oh good. Brian is here. "Brian! How're you?"

"Fine?" He frowned, looking at Adakiel in the corner. "Who's the kid? Do I need to kick him out?"

Adakiel scowled, rising to his feet. "No no. We're good." I cut in before he could speak. There's no telling what he was going to say. I've only met one angel before and he's a little... Aggressive. "This is Michael's," Think Medusa! "Little brother! Yeah this is Aidan. He's just visiting. Said he really wanted to meet me."

"Oh," Brian blinked, "I didn't realize you and Michael were at the meet the family stage already. Well as long as he's not some creep he can stay. Just don't mess with the customers, kid."

Adakiel nodded, slowly sitting back down. "I assure you the only thing I am here to observe is Medusa. I am very curious about the woman my *brother* is spending time with." Oh good. I was worried he would call me out.

"There are more of them? *Jesus*." Poor Brian. He looked so troubled at the mere thought. "Well I'm glad you're alright. We're in the homestretch now."

Four hours later, and I think I have officially lost my title as the Virtue of Patience. Adakiel had stared at me the whole time without saying a single word. He restocked the shelves with me. He waited silently while I went to the back to get more inventory, and followed me when I stocked those items as well. I offered to let him stay at the front while I went through and straightened some miscellaneous items, but he declined. Apparently when he told Michael he'd watch me, he meant like a hawk. I've had to pee for an hour! Adakiel wouldn't let me go by myself because, and I quote, "Women climb out of bathroom windows every day." This bathroom doesn't even have a window!

"Michael!" Before I could even comprehend what I was doing, I was throwing my arms around his neck. Michael caught me effortlessly, albeit more than a little confused.

"Medusa. Are you ill?" Michael asked holding me.

"Nope! Just happy to see you." I don't think I could ever handle Adakiel for as long as I handle Michael. At least Michael talks to me. "Please don't leave me with him again."

Michael laughed, "You are free to go, brother." He bent over to set me back on my feet. "I thought you would like Adakiel. He is one of the more quiet of my brethren."

"He's *very* quiet. So quiet that he was driving me crazy. I don't think I can be called patient anymore. He just followed me around silently the *whole time*." It was maddening. Michael just raised a brow at me. "I'm just glad you're back, okay? Is it wrong to say that I missed you?"

"Oh, ew." I jumped, turning to face Brian. He held his hands over his eyes, "Are you two being a couple?"

"No." Michael answered, "I thought you said being - *ahem* - romantic at your job would get you fired?" Where did he- Why would he *say* something like that?! I never said that! We never even talked about anything like that! Michael stepped toward me with a playful look in his eyes. I don't like that at all.

"Yes! Yes! That is now true! No couple stuff." Brian quickly cut in before Michael could reach me. Thank goodness.

Michael just sighed, letting me go, "Rules are rules, I suppose. I'll be good." I frowned, watching him go back to being the stoic man he always was. What just happened?

"Thank you. You about ready to close up, Medusa?" Brian asked, looking over the register.

"I'm never ready to leave this place, Brian. I love it here." My boss just snorted. Even Michael rolled his eyes. They must think I'm joking. I'm really not. This place is much better than home most of the time.

"Right. Well you go clock out, I'll take care of everything up here. Ah, Michael you can't go in the back..." Michael nodded, moving to stand by the doors. Brian shot me a wide eyed glance making me laugh. I guess he just realized he left himself with Michael. I'll have to hurry before Brian has a full scale panic attack from standing by Michael for too long.

When I came back, Brian looked significantly paler, and Michael seemed as bored as always. Brian basically shoved me out the door, so he could lock up the store. Michael must really make him uncomfortable. Brian used to hate closing up alone.

"I make that human uncomfortable, don't I?" Michael mused, easily walking ahead of me. He almost seemed proud.

I jogged, trying to keep pace with him. He didn't slow even a little bit. Chivalry really is dead. "Immensely." Michael waited impatiently on the driver's side of the car while my horribly short legs made up the distance. I climbed into the car with a quiet huff.

Michael scowled at me as he took his seat, "Must you walk so slow? You already get off work so late, then you take hours to make it to the car. It's like you don't want to train at all today."

I don't. I really *really* don't. Every time we 'train' I end up bruised and exhausted. "You know," I pointedly looked out the window, avoiding his gaze. "I think there's some things you could learn from me."

The giant scoffed obnoxiously, "What in the world could you possibly teach me?"

"How do be more *patient* seems like a good place to start." I didn't have to look to know he was rolling his eyes at me.

"I am the Chief of Heaven's Angels. I commanded my father's forces, and personally made sure my fallen brother's *lapdog* was sent back to the depths of Hell where he belongs. Believe me, Medusa, there is nothing I need to learn from *you*." Well there goes my joke. I sighed, resting my forehead on the cool window.

Chapter Six

I sighed, taking a seat by the quiet brook. Michael was inside somewhere. I don't know what he was doing, and at this point I don't really care. I'm not angry with him. I'm just tired. He's been in a mood for the past couple days. I have that lunch with Karma in a couple days, so that's something to look forward to.

"Medusa!" I definitely flinched at the sound of his voice. Darn it. Michael's shadow loomed over me, ruining the peaceful slightly warm atmosphere that Telluride had gifted me with today. I huddled into myself, not looking at him. He could have at least brought me a jacket if he was going to make it snow. "*What* are you doing?"

"Enjoying the peacefulness of my home." I replied, still not looking away from the water. I dipped my fingers in the brook, letting the water run over my finger tips.

Michael growled behind me. I guess he doesn't like me being indifferent to him. He sat down beside me with an incredibly loud huff. "We are supposed to be training today. You still haven't got a tree to lose a branch. You *have* to get stronger."

"Why?" It was a simple question. One that Michael didn't seem to have the answer to. Maybe I should start counting how long it takes him to speak again. He'd probably yell at me. I don't want that. He can be very loud when he wants to be.

"You don't need to know why. What matters is that it needs to happen. You have to get stronger before the other Virtues are found." That didn't last as long as I thought it would.

But since he seems a little more open to talk about everything, "So," I shifted toward him, finally looking at him. He looks as grumpy as usual. "What is the plan when we find the other Virtues?"

"To gather and train them. The same as I am doing with you." He gave me a blank look. "I thought that would be obvious."

"It was." Is he sure his goal isn't to *break* us? I can't be the Virtue of Patience if he kills all of my patience, and he is doing a *spectacular* job. I tugged on my ponytail, and pressed on. "I mean what is the plan after that. What do you plan on us *doing*?"

"That is not something you need to know at the moment." Just because I don't *need* to know doesn't mean I wouldn't like to know. It is my future, after all. I doubt that would change Michael's mind though. Suddenly, Michael straightened, his brows furrowing. "My father has requested me. I will return shortly."

Before I could reply, the little bursts of light appeared over his body. It was as if his body was being swallowed by little stars. I had to block the radiance with both hands before he accidentally blinded me. Well, I hope it was accidentally. No more than twenty seconds later, the light was gone taking Michael with it. Well, that was interesting. Will I be able to do something like that?

If I do make it there, it'll be much later. Wind needs to be my main focus. Michael said I need to be stronger before we meet the other Virtues. Maybe I should practice my magic while he's not here to yell at me. I pushed myself up from the ground, and made my way to my room. Dad was asleep on the couch when I came through. An old football game was still playing on the tv, but I left it on. Hopefully it will keep him asleep while I practice my magic.

I shut my bedroom door, and settled into the middle of my bed. Okay, small steps first. There's no need to push myself too fast without a certain someone breathing down my neck. Lucky for me, I had left a book on my dresser some time ago. It wasn't by anything breakable either, so I could just get started. Thank you, past me.

"Okay," I sighed, letting the breath take my tension away. I can do this. Keeping my eyes open this time, I focused on the book. Every other time I've used my magic, I've had my eyes closed. Maybe if I keep my eyes open, I will have a better chance of succeeding. I centered my focus on my breathing. I could feel the crisp air as it entered my lungs, and the warmth of the air as it left me.

I could feel the air in the room as if it was breathing with me. There wasn't any form of negative energy disrupting my focus, or anyone to make me feel stressed. It was actually *really* nice. I miss how much alone time I used to have. No, Medusa. That is not what we're focusing on right now.

Right. I gathered some of the air around me, and focused it on the book. If I could just get it to move *a lit-* "Oh no!" Oh no. No no no no no.

"*What was that noise?*" My father roared from the living room.

I cringed, "I fell!" *Please* believe me. I've never been very good at lying. My father didn't reply, though, so I guess I was believable enough. Now, what to do about that...

忍

It's been two hours, and I've come up with *nothing*. Not a single plausible solution. "Where's Michael when I need him?" I'm not usually a whiner. At least, I try not to be. There's always a positive side. That's what my mom believed, and I try to stay true to that. But, I can't find any positive side of this.

"Why is there a hole in your closet door?" I squeaked, whipping around to face the frost giant that *definitely* wasn't in my room a few minutes ago. "Medusa, stop gaping at me. What happened to the door?"

"Well," I twisted my hands in front of me, looking away from him. He didn't seem particularly mad at me, but that could change. He was going to be furious when he found out I was practicing magic without his supervision. "I was practicing my magic while I didn't have any distractions. I was going to see if I could push the book that was on the side of my dresser, and make it fall on the floor. I must've pushed too hard though, because it went through my closet door, and a replacement door is really expensive, and I can't afford it, and I definitely can't tell my dad that I broke it, so now-"

"Stop talking." Michael grumbled, effectively shutting me up. He's definitely mad. The angel moved toward the closet door to peer through the giant hole. After a few moments of deafening silence, he hummed, straightening back to his full height. "I didn't think you were capable of that much force. I will fix the door. Your father will never know it was broken. "

"Really?" He'd do something like that for me?

"Yes. I have to return to my own father. Practice your magic while I am gone. Find out why you were so much stronger here. I will return."

"Wait, Micha-" Too late. Well, at least the door was getting fixed, I suppose.

忍

"Medusa." I jumped, turning to face Michael. He'd been gone for about day now. He'd fixed my door while I was sleeping, but didn't wake me up. I should probably tell him what creepy means. "Get dressed. My father wants to speak with you." God?! Wait, what's wrong with what I'm wearing? Michael scowled at me, "You cannot wear those unreasonably short shorts to meet with the AllFather."

They're not that short, but I got up to change anyway. I slipped on a floral accordion skirt and a light pink shirt with some flats. That should be nice enough. I'd wear it to church, if I ever went to church. I came out of the closet to show Michael. The frosty giant gave me a once over before nodding, "Good enough." He held out an arm for me to loop mine through, "Do not scream. Do not let go. Do *not* pet me."

White fog completely overtook us, making me clutch him tighter. Why would he think I would let go? I can't see my own feet! Maybe I should just keep my eyes closed. That's a good plan. I went ahead and buried my face into Michael's arm too, just to be sure. I'm not sure what this magic is called, but it's nauseating.

"You can open your eyes now, Medusa." He growled, gently prying me from him.

I blinked, using my hand to shield away most of the light. Why is it so bright in here? Michael was blocking out some of the light, but it seemed to radiate from every surface. "Oh my god..." Michael's wings were back. They looked so soft.

"Yes?" I turned to see a man with long white blonde hair, and cold golden eyes that chilled me to the bone. I thought Michael was the most apathetic person I've ever met. This guy is something else entirely. He was wearing a crisp white three piece suit that was almost as bright as the rest of the room, and kept his hands folded in front of him. *This* is Yhwh? "Medusa, correct?"

"Y-Yes, sir." He nodded, coming closer. Michael was silent beside me with his arms folded. He seemed more tense than usual.

"You're smaller than I imagined. Much more... *Fragile.* Like a porcelain doll." Maybe creepy is just the theme for today. My eyes darted to Michael, but he wasn't looking at me. He was in full statue mode. I would've felt less alone if he wasn't here. Yhwh was standing in front of me now, the white reflecting so much, I had to turn away. His hand grasped my chin, facing me to look at him, "Let's stick to Yhwh when you speak to me, child. God is a term humans came up with."

"Okay." I hadn't been talking about him when I said it, I was talking about Michael's wings, but I don't think he cared.

"Now, I heard you've been struggling with developing your magic. Why is that?"

I frowned. How am I supposed to know? "I don't know. I'm trying, though."

Yhwh scowled at me, gripping my chin even tighter, "That isn't good enough. We are strengthening your training. You need to be stronger." He snapped his hand away from me, taking a step back. "Michael, this way."

Michael followed him toward the far end of the room, his unreasonably soft wings brushing me as he passed. I was left to stand there alone while Yhwh spoke to him, "You have failed me with this Michael. She's *weak*. I could snap her in half with minimal effort. I told you to make her stronger. Her magic signature is that of a basic human! Perhaps I should've chosen one of your brothers to train her instead. You obviously cannot handle training her." I wonder if he knows sound carries in an empty stone room, and I can hear everything he's saying about me. What was the point of walking away from me at all?

"No, Father. I can do this. Medusa is improving every day. She just needs time." He thinks I'm improving? That made me smile. I fiddled with my skirt, slowly walking in a circle. Heaven certainly seems boring. Shouldn't there be other angels here?

"Time?" Yhwh scoffed, "I am running out of patience, Michael. Fix her or I will find someone who can."

"Yes, Father."

"Medusa," Yhwh called. He was scowling at me, "I expect better." He waved his hand in my direction, making the white fog come back to cover me completely.

"Father! She can't-"

Then he was gone. Or rather, I was. I landed back in my room on my feet, but fell almost immediately as my legs gave out. I hit my bedroom floor with a thud, whacking my head on my bed frame on the way down. This has been an exhausting day. Oh no. I slapped my hand over my mouth and darted to the bathroom. Hopefully my own father can't hear me throwing up. I don't think I can handle anything else right now.

Once I was done and could stand without falling back over, I brushed my teeth and washed my face, and went to lay in my bed. I don't have any plans today. What's a nap going to hurt? I do know one thing. I am so sick of magic. Literally.

忍

'Hey girlie! Are you busy tonight? I was thinking a mini girl's night at Serenity. I'm buying.'

It was May. I thought she'd given up inviting me to her girl's nights after I said no half a million times. Normally, I'd say no because I was broke or had work the following day or just tired, but after my little meeting today I could really use a fun night. Plus, I'm off tomorrow so I can stay up a little later tonight.

'Don't panic, but I would love to. What's Serenity?'

'Yesssssss it's about damn time. Nightclub. I'll swing by and grab you around 8?'

'I'll be ready!'

I'll need to be ready at seven, just in case she arrives early. Oh my God. What am I supposed to wear to a nightclub? Why did I toss my phone away? Don't let me down internet. Okay, well I don't have a skirt that tight. Ooh! I have jeans kind of like that, and I *think* I own a crop top. I have to have at least one. Found it! Yeah, I bought this without unfolding it so I didn't know it was a crop top and was too embarrassed to return it. Being socially awkward had to work out for me sometime, right?

Now, what to do with this blonde mop? Maybe a messy updo. Those are in style... I think. Why did I agree to this? I don't know how to go to a nightclub. Too late now, Medusa. You already committed. Now, go find your heels, and pray they still fit.

'Here. I'm a little early, so don't worry about rushing.'

Already? Oh god! It's fifteen till eight! I'm never this bad with time. I grabbed my bag, and rushed out the door.

"Where the hell are you going?" For the first time in possibly forever, I ignored him.

May beamed at me as I climbed into the car, "Wooo! Well don't you look like sin." I laughed. She looked much better than me. In fact, she was dressed almost identical to the photos I looked at for reference before I got dressed. "Ready for your first girl's night, Medusa?"

"Ready as I'll ever be. Do I look okay?" I fiddled with the hem of my shirt. May certainly looked much more sexy than I did.

"You look great! I didn't know you owned crop tops. Oh, look in the grocery bag in the floorboard. I got you something. Now," She held a hand up, pausing my movement. Her blue eyes were shining with sincerity, "You don't have to use them, but if you want them they're brand new and all yours."

I peered at her, reaching for the bag. It wasn't from Whittle Corner. It was from an actual beauty supply store that I know we don't have in town. Where did she get this? Inside the bag was mascara, eyeliner, a beautiful lipstick, and a pallet of eye shadow.

"Oh wow, May. I can't accept this." I put them back in the bag as softly as I could. They looked expensive, I'd hate to mess them up. "I wouldn't even know how to use them."

"You've never done your makeup?" She asked, incredulous. She couldn't look at me since she was driving, but it was clear she wanted to. "Do you want me to do yours? I'm pretty good. I mean, I'm not a professional or anything, but I get by."

I could tell that much the first time I met her. It never looked like too much when she did it. Last time I attempted makeup, I looked like I let a four year old do it. "Would you?"

"Hell yeah!" She didn't mind me laughing at her enthusiasm. In fact, she even laughed with me. Michael would never do that. Maybe she's right. I do need a girl's night.

We pulled up outside a cool looking restaurant called Embers a few minutes later. I thought we were going to a place called Serenity? "Alright, hand over the baggie, and face me." I did as I was told and May got to work.

"Hey, May?" She hummed, tilting my face up a little. An intense look of concentration had settled on her face as she applied the makeup. I felt a little bad for disturbing her train of thought. "I thought we were going to a place called Serenity?"

"Hmm?" Her eyes refocused on mine, losing some of the intensity. "Oh! We're meeting Kat and Zelda here before we head over. It's right next door. That's why I parked a little over instead of right by the door or Ember. It's always good to eat something before a night out. Close your eyes for this next part."

I closed my eyes, trying not to react to how weird the little brush felt. I'm not used to this at all. "Kat and Zelda are your friends, I take it?"

"Yup!" She chirped, popping the 'p' in time with the brush stroke off my eye lid. What is she doing? "Keep them closed. Time for liner. You'll love the girls though. Pretty sure they think I made you up." She laughed, "All done. You can open your eyes. Do you want to do the lipstick?"

"Yes, please." I took the offered tube, and turned to my visor. Oh wow. I looked... Really pretty. May must be some sort of wizard to pull this off. My eyes looked a lot more green than usual, too. I applied the red lipstick as well as I could, and smiled at May.

"Beautiful! Ready?" She shimmed at me before turning the car off, and hopping out.

"As ready as I'll ever be..." I murmured, getting out myself. It was a warm night for Fall in Colorado, and we weren't the only people out enjoying it. This place is packed! All of the rounded furniture were shades of black and grey, while the lighting that was hidden somewhere in the walls cast a red glow over the place. "I can see why it's called Embers."

May nodded, "Pretty cool, huh? They have some of the best food. Oh, hey," She paused, turning to face me. Her blue eyes were intimidatingly serious - I didn't realize she could look so serious. She almost resembled Michael. "I meant it when I said that I'm buying, so no unreasonably small meal because you feel bad. Actually order some food or I'm getting you a sixteen ounce steak."

"They make sixteen ounce steaks?" That seemed way too big to be real.

May pursed her lips. I think she was trying not to laugh at me, but she held firm. "I'll make them put two on the plate. Just don't worry about the money, okay. I know how you are."

Well, she did have a point. I sighed, "I will do my best." Especially since she said the two steak thing. Steaks are crazy expensive! No way can I let her spend that much on me. I don't even think I can eat that much either, so I'd feel twice as bad.

"That is all I ask. Remember, tonight is a fun night. Oh look!" She pointed a little past the hostess stand. The hostess seemed startled at my friend's outburst, instantly making May put her hand down. "Sorry! Our friends are a few tables behind you."

"Oh! You can head on back. Enjoy your meal!" The sweet girl motioned us past the stand. She couldn't have been older than eighteen. I think I was a hostess when I was sixteen, if I remember correctly. That is definitely a job I don't miss.

"Hey! You ready to relax?" A girl about my height with shoulder length curled blonde hair wiggled her eyebrows at May. "Oh! You must be Medusa! It's so nice to meet you!"

She pulled me into a hug, swaying us in space for a moment. "Well aren't you sweet! It's so nice to meet you... Kat?" Kat is an upbeat name, right?

"Oh, no." She laughed, "I'm Zelda. This is Kat."

She waved her hand to the other person at the table. A girl with a black faux hawk hairstyle with the top combed forward, and fierce honey brown eyes wearing a blue tailored pantsuit and stilettos raised her whiskey glass at me, "Are you going to make them stand all day, Z?"

Zelda moved back to her seat, gesturing for us to take the remaining two. I settled into the seat beside Kat while May took the seat beside Zelda. "It's nice to meet you, too, Kat. You know, I think I know someone you'd like a lot." She looked like the kind of person Karma would like.

She quirked a brow at me, taking another sip of her drink. "Not a big fan of people." Yup. Karma would like her. I just know it. "So, Medusa, what made you finally join us for girls' night?"

How do I word this without magic, or God, or archangels? "Men are exhausting." It came out more like a question, but all three girls nodded along with me.

"The guy at the park? He does seem a little stoic to be with you. You need someone happy. Not always smiling, but certainly not so grumpy. Sorry," She waved her hand, "I don't want to butt in."

"Wait, wait." Zelda cut in, pushing two plates to the center of the table, "Crab Cakes and Beef Wellington, help yourself. Do you have a picture of this boyfriend? Just so we can all weigh in."

Oh. Oh dear. I don't have a picture of him. He's supposed to be my boyfriend and I don't have a picture of him? "Let me see if I can find a good one.

He doesn't really like them." I pulled my phone out of my pocket to see a message from a number I didn't know I had.

'I saved my number in your ridiculous mini box since you always have it on you so you can't pretend to ignore me.'

Oh please, please reply quickly. **'Send me a picture of you that looks like I took a cute picture of my boyfriend. Please!'**

'Why aren't you training!' Well, I gave myself away, but he sent a picture! It even looked like I took it at the park. He wasn't smiling, but that would be expecting a lot. I enlarged it, and showed the girls.

"Goddamn," Kat hummed, "I don't even like men."

"I do! He is very fun to look at. Why no smile, though?" Zelda asked, tilting her head slightly.

"Michael doesn't really like to smile. Or laugh." Or have any sort of fun really.

"He did seem to like Medusa when I met him. They do couples meditating in the park. He even calls her 'love' as a pet name."

Zelda cooed at that, "That is so sweet. I like the long blond hair. Does he wear it down a lot?"

"Why does that matter?" Kat cut in, "What did he do to make you so exhausted?"

I sighed, taking one of the Beef Wellington from the plate, "He's helping me get healthier." That's believable, right? It's mostly true. "And he's just pushing me a little too hard. Have you ever tried Krav Maga or Northarn Shaolin? They're awful. Truly the worst thing I have ever done."

Kat frowned, finally setting her drink down. She actually turned to face me. Does this count as progress? "He looked at you - little, fragile Medusa - and thought you should try *martial arts*? That's so dumb. You look like you can barely handle a bag of jumbo marshmallows."

"Mildly offensive, Kat. Tone it down." May warned, "Do we have a waitress?"

Kat groaned, rolling her eyes, "Yes. One second." Her eyes scanned the restaurant floor for a moment before nodding. "She's on the way, and definitely into me."

Zelda and May just rolled their eyes. I guess they're used to her antics. It was an odd change of pace, but I don't mind it. I actually like Kat's confidence and air of superiority. Michael would hate her. *A lot*.

"Hello! So sorry for the wait!" A perky waitress who had to be a few years younger than all four women at the table. Kat was correct, though. She was certainly the waitress' main focus. "Can I get you something to drink?"

May and I gave our drink orders. All three girls ordered food as well. I quickly chose a burger that looked delicious with some sweet potato casserole and broccoli. May smiled at me when I was done. I guess I passed.

"Be honest," May rested her head on her hand, "Do you eat anything that's not burgers?"

I laughed, "Not usually. I do love burgers. Michael hates that I eat so many." That's a little bit of an understatement. Michael *loathes* hamburgers. I think Brian is afraid of death if he brings me a burger again.

'Where are you? Are you training?'

"*Good lord*. Is that the boyfriend?" Kat asked, waving her crab cake at me. "Fuck him. For one night, turn off the phone, ignore your boyfriend that seems *way* to fucking overbearing, and have fun."

"*Kat*," Zelda snapped, "Too harsh. Seriously, we talked about how to talk to people." She flicked Kat's hand, still glaring at her. Is this a mom friend? I think I'm finally understanding that phrase.

Kat rolled her eyes, taking a long sip of her drink. The waitress came back with a tray of shots. Who ordered shots? Judging from the expressions on the girls' faces, they were also confused. Kat pursed her lips, "We didn't order jäger shots, because we're not in college."

"Oh," The waitress blinked, clearly not expecting Kat's tone. "That table over there sent them over."

We turned to see a table of men in pastel collared shirts smiling widely at us. Kat made a disgusted noise, "I'm way too gay for this." I laughed despite myself. Kat just winked back at me. How have we never met? Well, I know how, but I'm definitely regretting being such a hermit.

"Don't encourage her." May sighed. She turned to the waitress, smiling sweetly, "Can you throw those in the trash? Or give them to the table that ordered them? We won't drink them, and *someone* has a *very* protective boyfriend who *really* won't like her accepting these." Was she talking about me?

The waitress' eyes widened and she nodded rapidly, "I completely understand. Your food should be out shortly." She took the tray of shots and darted over to the men's table.

Kat nodded, leaning back in her chair again, "The one good thing about you having an ape of a boyfriend, Medusa. Gets rid of guys like that."

"Do you deal with guys like that a lot?" I'd never experienced anything like that. Then again, I don't really go out all that much.

"Yes." Kat rolled her eyes.

Zelda gave her a flat look, "They're not all bad. Kat just doesn't like men." Kat rolled her eyes again. She unbuttoned one of the top buttons on her blouse, and pulled it to the side to reveal a pink, white, and red flag. It looked like a pride flag of some sort. "We *get* it." *Oh*. It must be her pride flag. That makes sense.

"But," May cut in, holding up a hand. "Tonight is a Girl's Night. No boyfriends, and no boys."

Zelda sighed, *"Fine."*

"If you're interested in them, they were probably no good anyway, Z." That got a crab cake thrown at Kat. Zelda just scowled as her friend adeptly caught the small cake in her mouth.

"Alright," A cheerful waiter appeared at the table, "We have a barbecue burger with sweet potato casserole and broccoli." This looked *amazing*. I was practically drooling. Now *this* is one of those greasy monstrosities Michael would hate. I should send him a picture. No, I shouldn't. He could probably track me down with minimal effort. Kat got a steak with a lobster tail while May and Zelda got some sort of fish that I couldn't identify. "Anything else?"

We declined. Well, May, Zelda, and I declined. Kat was already eating her lobster tail. I really hope she gets to meet Karma some day. They'd get on like a house fire. At least, I think they would. Who knows, Karma liked me, so maybe they wouldn't get along since they seem pretty similar.

"You okay, Medusa? You zoned out for a moment." May called me back into focus.

"Oh!" I blinked at her, trying to get out of my thoughts. I have to remember to not go quiet when I'm around people. This isn't work, they actually want me to talk to them. I just worry about saying something stupid. "Sorry I get a little lost in thought sometimes. This is delicious!"

"You're okay." She laughed. She'd made significant progress with her fish plate, and her mashed potatoes were completely gone. I should hurry. "You're resting face is sad looking. It's like the opposite of RBF."

"What's RBF?"

That got me a shocked look from everyone else at the table. Kat even paused eating, "Resting Bitch Face." She explained, laughing a little. "You don't get out much, do you?"

"Not really." I shrugged, "I work a lot. That's why I'm usually too tired to come to these. I'm glad I'm here though. I like you two." Zelda beamed back at me, but didn't reply since her mouth was full.

Kat smiled, "I kinda like you too. You're like some sort of kitten."

"*Kat.*" Zelda scolded, holding a hand over her mouth.

"It's not an insult! Kittens are cute!" I laughed. She wasn't bothering me, honestly. There are worst things to be compared to than a kitten. Kat waved at me, "See? Medusa doesn't mind!"

"You could steal food off her plate, and she'd apologize that her plate wasn't closer to you." May replied, rolling her eyes. "She's extremely nice and compassionate. Don't be an ass." May pushed her chair back, and stood up. "I'll be right back. *Behave.*"

Kat scoffed, crossing her arms. Her eyes darted to my sweet potatoes one more time. I pushed the small ceramic dish over to her. I couldn't eat anymore anyway. There's no way I can handle a sixteen ounce steak.

"Seriously?" She quirked a brow at me.

"Yes," I laughed, "I can't eat any more."

"*Yessssss.*"

"Goddamn it, Kat. I was gone for five minutes." May scowled down at Kat. That was fast.

"She gave it to me!"

"I did give it to her." I backed her up. Kat waved at me like 'See? I'm telling the truth.' May just scowled harder.

"Fine. Does that mean you're ready to go?" May let it go. "I already paid the check." Oh. Dang it. I was going to insist on paying for my meal or at least covering the tip. I thought she was going to the bathroom not paying the bill. Judging from her smirk, she was well aware.

"*May!*" Zelda and Kat scolded at the same time. Huh, I didn't think they agreed on anything.

"That means drinks are on me. Yours too, Medusa." Kat smoothly got up from the table, setting the napkin over her plate. She held a hand out to help me get up. I didn't need it, but took it anyway. Once I was standing, Kat swung her arm over my shoulders. "Cute outfit. How gay are you?"

"Seriously?" Zelda gave her a flat look, pushing past her.

"*What?*" Kat tried to make an innocent face, but failed when a wide smile spread over her face. Now I have to wonder if she's like this when Zelda isn't here to agitate.

"See?" May pointed to an orange sign once we made it outside. "It's right there."

"Oh." How did I miss that? That sign is huge. Plenty of people were already parked, and heading inside the nightclub.

Music greeted us immediately. There were people *everywhere*. Holy cow. Kat, who's arm was still slung over my shoulders, seemed perfectly at ease in this loud atmosphere. Then again, with her confidence, wardrobe, and general attitude that shouldn't be such a surprise.

"Oh my god. Kat, is that you?" Kat froze, her arm slipping off my shoulders. She also looked significantly paler.

"Hey, *you.*" Uh oh. That can't be good.

The girl's sultry smile morphed into a much more angry expression, "You don't know my name, do you? I guess that's not surprising for someone who ghosted me."

"I didn't ghost you. People don't talk after one night stands. That's how it goes." Sounds normal to me, but what do I know? I've never done anything like that. This girl didn't seem to agree, though. "Why are you mad?"

"I thought we had something special!"

"You didn't." Zelda deadpanned, pushing herself in between Kat and the girl. "There's nothing special. She's just a pro at impressing coeds. You promised me a drink, Kat."

"I promised you several, actually." That got a smile out of Zelda. May appeared beside me, nodding me along. I followed perhaps a little too eagerly. If I was with the group maybe that girl wouldn't yell at me next. I haven't done anything to her, but I am here with Kat. We got to the bar, where there were two barstools available. "Medusa, you're on a stool."

I hopped on the stool Kat pulled out, turning so I could still see the girls. Zelda got on the other stool, with Kat and May standing behind us. I'm assuming they were the ones standing due to their much taller stature than ours. Zelda waved the bartender down with a bright smile. The man smiled back, and motioned he'd be right over.

"Oh, but I flirt with the waitress and get in trouble." Kat snorted, "What're you drinking, Kitten?"

"Oh, I don't drink."

"Really?" Zelda looked completely taken aback. She frowned slightly, "What if it is a really weak drink? I know a good one. Not very much alcohol, just enough to make you feel a little lighter."

I shook my head, "No, thank you. It's not really my thing." I already know there's at least a slight addictive gene in my DNA. I don't need to play with fire.

"Ooh," May tapped her chin, "Have you ever had a Shirley Temple?" I shook my head. I've heard of them, but I'm pretty sure they have alcohol in them. "Do you like ginger ale?"

"Not particularly..."

"What about coke?" Kat asked. May looked at her, the confusion clear on her face. "It's a drink similar to the Shirley Temple with zero alcohol, but instead of ginger ale, it has coke." That sounds interesting. Kat fist pumped at my agreement. "It's called a Roy Rogers. I assume you're ordering?"

Zelda smiled sweetly at Kat, snatching the taller woman's card. They have such an odd relationship. May just rolled her eyes at them. I suppose she's use to all this. The Dj said something over the speaker system before shifting to a much louder song. The crowd on the dance floor cheered, easily dancing to the new beat. May and Zelda were nodding along to the music, with May even dancing in place.

May leaned in so I could hear her, "I'm going to dance. I love this song! Do you wanna come?"

"Oh! Um, maybe later?" I'm going to need some time before I'm brave enough to wade into that monstrosity.

"Okay. Be back later!" She was dancing long before she reached the dance floor.

Zelda shook her head, "That girl and her music." Then the bartender was here, and Zelda became a whole different person. She sat up straighter, she was smiling brightly, and blinking much more than she should be. I suppose it worked though, because when the bartender finally left to fill our order he looked a little dazed.

Kat just rolled her eyes, "This is the only reason you come out. Oh, I see a table. I'm going to sit down. I'm going to sit down. You coming?"

I hesitated, looking at Zelda. I shouldn't leave her alone over here with this many people... "You're okay, Medusa. I work best alone anyway." Whatever that means. I did get the message that she wanted me gone though, driven home by the raised blonde eyebrows.

Kat walked confidently through the club, seeming to know exactly where she was going. I don't know how she saw any tables over all these bodies, but then again, she has to be six feet tall. She slapped the table when we reached it. It was a tall table with tall barstools that Kat slid on with ease. She laughed watching me struggle onto the stool that came up to my chest even in heels.

"Glad you enjoyed yourself." I huffed, finally on my stool. Kat continued to laugh into her hand. "What are you, seven feet tall?"

"I'm six, one if you must know. Are you tall enough to ride any adult rides at Six Flags?" She jested back, pulling my stool closer to her. "I can barely hear you from how far down you are from me."

"Alright, alright. I give. You are a superior tall person."

"Damn right." She winked, "So, how do you feel being away from the boyfriend?"

How *do* I feel? Michael had become such a large part of my life so quickly, and he *did* end up fixing my door. He can also be horribly mean and impatient at times. I sighed, resting my head in my palms. How do I answer that? *Do* I miss him? "I guess I miss him a little, but he would hate this entire environment."

"You sure about that, dear? Your eyes scan the club every five minutes. Looking for some light blue eyes?" She waggled her eyebrows at me. "It's okay to admit it. You get no judgement with me. I get it."

"You get it? Aren't you the gayest gay to ever gay?"

She guffawed, "Hell yeah I am!" She shook her head at me, still smiling. "But that isn't what I meant. May doesn't talk about it, because it isn't her story to tell, but she alluded to you being a bit of a loner. Couple that knowledge with the name Medusa, I have a general gist of what your life has been so far. If you ever need anyone to talk about anything, don't be afraid to give me a call. There are some things people like May and Zelda can't understand."

Deep emotion reflected in her light brown eyes. Kat's eyes grew hazy as she stared down at the table. It was a look I recognized well. "Hey, Kat?" She hummed, blinking at me. She was still slightly lost in thought, but seemed to be coming back. "Kat is short for something, isn't it?"

She laughed once, ruffling her hair. "Hecate, actually." Oh. *Oh.* Now I understand. "Don't tell the girls, though. They think my name is Katherine. Once I suffered through middle school, and got to high school I figured Katherine would be easiest. The teachers and staff agreed that it would help ease my issues with my classmates."

"Hecate was a witch, right?"

She shook her head, "That's what everyone thinks. She's a goddess in Greek Mythology. She's the goddess of magic, witchcraft, the night, moon, ghosts, and necromancy. *But* because of the magic, and the witchcraft, and necromancy people tend to associate her with a bunch of negative stuff." She coughed, "I'm sure that sounds familiar."

"Yeah," I scoffed, "I'm glad you had a nickname, though. Medusa doesn't really have any nicknames." Besides 'Gorgon' which Mac loves so much.

"For real." She sighed, looking past me. "Here comes Zelda. Let's table this, yeah?" I nodded, watching a smile appear on her face. Gone was any trace of the sadness that she showed me a moment ago. In fact, it was like she completely closed up. Became a different person. "That is *much* more than you ordered!" She teased.

Zelda slid the tray on the table before hopping up on the stool with practiced grace. Benefits of coming to bars more frequently, I guess. She handed out drinks with a smug smile, "Here is your purely non-alcoholic drink, Medusa. I double checked. Kat, double whiskey, and a Carthusian Sazerac which Lucas was very proud that he knew how to make."

"Lucas, huh?" Kat raised a brow, tasting the strange looking drink. "That's not bad. Very lemony. Want a taste, kitten? You can't taste the alcohol."

I thought it over, looking at the drink. Kat lifted it for me to sniff. It did smell a lot like lemon. "Hey you!" Another girl slipped onto the stool beside me. She had curled black hair, and wide dark brown eyes. She scooted close to me, leaning into me while laughing. Once she was close enough to whisper to me, the fear became prominent in her eyes, "Please pretend you know me. This guy won't leave me alone." My eyes flicked to the girls, both seeming to get the message. The girl leaned back and smiled widely again, "I couldn't see you for the life of me! Glad I finally found you!"

"Bout time too!" Kat laughed, "Though you should know better than to look for these shorties."

"Yeah," The girl laughed, "I should've kn-"

"So these are your friends, baby?" Some guy slung his arm around her shoulders, leaning in way too close for anyone to be comfortable. He seemed to be acting loopy, but... Wasn't.

"Yeah," This laugh was much more strained than before. Our new friend was radiating discomfort. "Thanks for helping me, but I'm with them now."

"Well, they know you're here, so let's go grab a drink." Does he not *see* how uncomfortable she is?

"The point was that she is with us - her friends that she came to hang out with - and that you were no longer needed. You can leave now." I interjected, tilting my head slightly. I studied him. Every few moments he'd wobble slightly, his voice would slur purposefully, and he'd sway closer to the girl's face. The rest of the table seemed to blink at me in shock.

Not unwanted guest though. His face transformed from his slimy smile to a sinister glare in my direction. Oh, there he is. I was right. "I am just trying to give Kali here a good time. Why are you trying to stop that? Don't you want your friend to have a good time?"

I scowled back at him. It was glaringly obvious that she *didn't* want to have a "good time" with him. Whatever that meant. "I don't know what makes you think spending time with a sleazy man who *pretends* to be drunk at a bar in an attempt to excuse his behavior is a good time. Which is still unacceptable even if you were inebriated - which you are *not*." I've seen drunk, and this man - if you can call him that - definitely was sober.

"Listen, bitch." Well he finally got off of Kali, but now had his hand wrapped firmly around my wrist.

"Hey, jackass." Kat's hand was on his wrist immediately, "I suggest you back the fuck off."

"I don't need some butch bitch and her bratty little whore telling me what to do." He snapped back. His other arm reared back, his hand already formed into a fist.

He was really planning on hitting us! When he was the one harassing someone! Suddenly, his grip was removed from my wrist as his hand shot to his own throat. The man gasped for air, dropping to the ground. Was this another poor acting job? What was the story this time? He wasn't eating or drinking anything, so it couldn't be choking. Why can't he just stand up and apologize? He could-

"Medusa." I blinked, looking up at the last person I wanted to see. Michael rubbed his hand over my back. Concern was so apparent in his eyes even I almost bought the boyfriend act. "Are you alright?"

"I'm fine. Why?"

"What the hell did you do to me, bitch?!" The man from before was back up and breathing... What did I do? Oh my god. My eyes shot to Michael. Surely that wasn't me. I wasn't even thinking about my powers! We both know that I can't use them without severe concentration... Unless I can, and just didn't know it. Oh no. "What are you? Some kind of *freak*?" His next attempt at a sentence was garbled as Michael grabbed him by the throat, lifting him off the ground with ease.

"If you must know, *pathetic insect,* she is an angel." He growled at the man. The air in the club dropped below freezing instantly, but that didn't stop the wet spot from spreading over the man's expensive looking slacks. Not that I could blame him for that. I can easily see how Michael became the general he's known to be. He wasn't yelling or cursing, but he didn't have to. His eyes said it all. They were several shades lighter than normal with a gold sheen, and held no warmth or humanity. They were the eyes of a man that had reaped more souls than I had ever met, and if this man didn't comply to whatever order he was about to be given he was going to be the next one. "I suggest you get as far away from me as possible within the next two minutes." He dropped him as quick as he grabbed him, and stayed standing in between him and me. To his credit, the shaking man with soiled pants landed on his feet and ran out of the club like his butt was on fire. Once he was out of sight, Michael turned back to me. He looked like the Michael I had come to know, and even smiled, "I leave you for five minutes and you start a fight at a nightclub?"

"Medusa!" May darted around the ice giant, and wrapped her arms around me. "Are you okay? What the hell happened? Who is this?" I choked out a laugh, and hugged her back. I caught Michael's eye over her shoulder, and gave him a weak smile. He just nodded. We'll definitely be having a conversation about this later. Though I should probably have him take me home now. Just in case I get emotional and my powers act up again...

May kept her arms wrapped around me as Kat and Zelda launched into the story, and introduced Kali who admitted that she told the not-drunk the wrong name and her real name is Amber. "Thank you, Medusa - right?" I pulled away from May, and nodded to her. She just smiled, not seeming put off in the slightest about my name. "Thank you so much. I'm sorry I got you into that situation. He wouldn't leave me alone, and I was getting nervous."

"As you should've been," Kat scoffed, "That guy was a grade A jackass. Hey, M, how did you know he was pretending to be drunk? I certainly thought he was." And here I thought she was determined to stick to 'kitten' as my nickname.

I shook my head, "It wasn't right. All of his moves seemed too calculated. Like he was planning them beforehand. It was very strange." I still don't get it.

Zelda coughed, "I actually heard about that, and now I'm mad I didn't catch it. Apparently it's a way to get girls to lower their guards because 'Duh the drunk guy wants to get more drinks' then he waits for you to drink with him and slips something in your drink. Good catch, Medusa." Where was she that she heard about something that awful? Goodness.

"So," Kat cut in, looking past May and me, "How about I buy you a drink for going all Superman for Medusa and me?"

Michael wasn't listening, though. He was scanning the area while scowling at every person he saw. I pulled away from May completely, and crossed to tap his arm. His eyes shot to mine, softening slightly, "Kat asked if she could get you a 'thank you' drink."

And he's scowling again. That was fast. "I don't drink, and you shouldn't be putting that poison in your body either."

"I haven't had any alcohol, if you must know." I stuck my tongue out at him.

He blinked back at me in shock, before his face relaxed back into a frown. That has to be its relaxed position by now. "*You* are a child. Do you need me to take you home?"

"No." I straightened. He was being nice because we're in public, but I just know he's furious with me for not training. "I'm having a good night with my friends - including Amber - but I'll see you tomorrow morning? I'm off tomorrow." He nodded, "Tomorrow then. Have a good night with your friends." He pressed a soft kiss to my temple and disappeared into the crowd.

Kat hummed, tapping her fingers on her chin. She was peering at me, "I think I approve of the boyfriend. That was pretty badass, showing up in the nick of time like that." I laughed. I'm glad he came, though I have no idea what he was doing here. Maybe he does have some kind of tracker on me. Oh, I don't like that. Regardless, I'm glad he showed up when he did. If he hadn't showed up that guy could've... He could've... I could have...

"Medusa! Come on." I looked back up to see four wide smiles. May rolled her eyes at me, "Stop daydreaming about the boyfriend. Girl's Night, remember?"

"I remember. Do you need a dance partner?"

"Hell yeah!"

Chapter Seven

Is it possible to have a hangover if you didn't drink? Like a people hangover, from being around too many people. If so, I definitely have one. My bed dipped, making me roll over till I hit the glacier that was sitting on my bed. I guess when Michael says morning, he means the early morning.

I opened my eyes only to immediately regret it. Evil man. Who opens every single curtains in a sleeping person's room? Evil people, that's who. "Are you going to pretend to be asleep forever?"

"I'm not pretending, I just can't open my eyes because my room is so bright. Can you close the curtains back, please?" I burrowed further into my blanket and his back to drive home my point. Maybe he'll show mercy.

Probably not, if his scoff was anything to go by. "Absolutely not. I need you awake for this conversation. We don't have a lot of time."

Now I'm awake. Darn him. "Why don't we have time? What's going on?"

Michael smirked at the sight of me fully sitting up, "I have to get back to my father, remember?" Oh. I should've thought of that. Michael moved back on my bed, pushing my pillows out of his way. Jokes on him. I'm willing to sleep on his shoulder too. With my blanket bunched around me, I scooted over the mattress to curl up against his side. He huffed, but didn't make me move, "We need to talk about what you did last night, Medusa." What are the chances that he just wants to hear about the good time I had after he left? "Specifically, when you used your powers to attempt murder." So zero, then.

I swallowed, curling tightly into myself. That's the *last* thing I wanted to talk about. "I didn't mean to."

"You were angry. That man made you so angry, your powers came out full force. If I hadn't shown up, you would have ki-"

"Please don't say that out loud." I really try to not cut him off, but I think I can make an exception today. "I had a good time with the girls, but once I got home and tried to go to sleep... I kept seeing him there." My dreams would flash between him gasping for air on the ground, his face when he was going to hit Kat because of me, the fear when he was being held by the throat, and, of course, Michael's eyes. A shudder racked down my spine.

"Are you cold? Do I need to grab you another blanket?" How can he be so different now?

"No, I'm alright. I don't know what happened last night. Honestly, I didn't even know that I was the one *doing* that until you showed up. How did you know where I was, anyway?" I still hadn't figured that out. It had nagged me most of the night.

"I felt your power surge, and came immediately in case you needed assistance. Which you did." That last bit wasn't really needed, but I doubt he could help himself. He shifted, drawing in a breath. "Medusa, I have concerns. Your powers surged with your anger, but anger is not meant to be your strength. If anything, Wrath is meant to be your weakness."

Wrath? That seems like a specific word choice... Michael didn't explain though. I pushed off of him, still keeping in my blanket cocoon, but now I could see his face. He did look concerned as he studied me, but that didn't make the staring any less unnerving. Finally, after what seemed like forever, he shrugged and got off the bed, "I need to return to Zion. Be careful, and actually *practice* your magic."

"Aye aye, captain!" I saluted. He gave me the best disgusted look I had ever seen, before sparkling away. Ooh he'd get so mad if he ever heard me call it that.

My phone chimed with a reminder, making me wobble to the other side of the bed to see it.

'Lunch with Karma'

Oh yeah! Good thing Michael left before my reminder. He'd blow a gasket if he knew who I was going to lunch with *and* where we were going. That being said, I don't have much time if I want to get there on time, but a quick shower is definitely needed.

I scanned *Steamie's* as I came through the door looking for any sight of Karma, but didn't find any. Good. I would hate to make her wait on me.

"Look what the cat dragged in. I thought you were banned from burgers." May laughed, leaning on the bar by the front door. "I'm surprised you're up. You looked exhausted last night."

"I was, and didn't really sleep so I still sort of am." I shrugged, "But I had already made plans today with a friend."

"A friend, huh? Did Kat bribe you with burgers? She seemed pretty taken with you last night." May didn't say it in a teasing way, but I could see a glint in her eyes that said she really wanted to.

"How would you know how Kat felt about me when you were distracted all night by a v-neck?"

She guffawed at me, "It was a very nice v-neck with even nicer abs, can you really blame me? Not that you'd care. Michael is built like a damn beast." She straightened moving to the hostess stand, "So, is it just the two of you or boyfriend, as well?"

"Just two, and if you could not mention this to Michael - like ever - that would be fantastic. Oh, and it's not Kat, though we did exchange numbers."

She raised a brow at me, but didn't say anything as she led me to a table toward the back, "Want anything to get you started? Chili, Mac and cheese, a drink?"

"I think I'll wait for her, actually. She should be here soon." May shrugged, and patted the table before wandering to her other tables. She had barely walked away when I saw a familiar ponytail walk through the front door. I stood up when she got close to me, and motioned for a hug. She laughed, wrapping her arms around me. "Hey! How's your arm? I know Michael grabbed you a little hard. I'm so sorry about him." When we pulled away I could fully see that both of her arms looked pretty normal, but that also begs the question of who wears a tank top in Colorado during Autumn? She didn't have a jacket on when she came through the door either. "I haven't ordered anything, yet. I wasn't sure what you'd want."

She waved off my question, her eyes scanning the menu, "My arm is much better, thank you. Any ideas on what I should order?" She seemed slightly bothered by the question, but maybe that's just the hunger. I know I can get cranky when I'm hungry.

Leaning forward, I pointed on her menu, "I prefer the steamie, but if you like barbecue sauce, I suggest the yeti." She nodded, making a deep humming sound. "However, I will cut you a part of mine to try for next time. They make their own sauce and it's *amazing*. Best burgers in town, hands down. Oh, and you have to get a milkshake. It'll change your life." Am I a little biased? Yes. But that doesn't make me wrong.

Karma smirked at me, finally lifted her head up, "You might be my new favorite person. Don't tell my best friend that's taking care of my house." I laughed, drawing an X over my heart. If someone is having to take care of her house, how long is she planning on being in town? "So, how's Michael and his sunshiny optimism?"

I was rolling my eyes before I could stop myself. I would approve of an optimistic Michael, but if this morning is anything to go off of, I'm not going to be seeing him until I'm dead. "I don't know." That's honest. Well... "Well, I do know he's never happy. He's been having some...Ah," How do you say this without saying he's arguing with God himself?! That's a crazy person thing to say. "Issues. With his dad." Good save. I hope.

Karma sighed, "Medusa, I need to be honest with you..."

"Hi! Welcome to *Steamie's*! Are you ready to order?" I could already tell May was having a field day now that she's seen my fitness model lunch buddy. We gave our orders. Mine coming with a warning look for her to not embarrass me. May promised to be back soon, giving Karma one more once over before going. Once she was out of

Karma's sight, she turned back to mouth at me, '*Holy shit!*' While making a fanning motion.

I rolled my eyes at her, and refocused on Karma. A dark look had taken over her face, and she was clenching her silverware in her fist. "Um, Karma?" I asked, reaching out to place my hand on hers. "Are you okay?"

She blinked, "What?" Her eyes darted down, and she released them as if they burned her. The previously normal silverware was now partially liquid on the table. She tossed a napkin over them, pulling on her ponytail.

I should've known this was too good to be true. *I need to be honest with you.* I should've expected him to send someone else to watch after me. Michael didn't react too kindly to her, he must not like other angels stepping in his space. "You're one of them, aren't you? Look, I'm cooperating with Michael, do I really need two angels hanging around?" I don't think I can handle that right now. Even if she is more tolerable than Adakiel.

"Oh no, I'm not an angel." She reached out to me, but didn't actually touch me. Her grey eyes seemed to plead with me, "Honestly."

"You're not?"

"Well, no. I am a demon, though." She laughed sheepishly, rubbing the back of her neck.

I'm sure me completely freezing up totally helped her awkwardness. Good job, Medusa. Maybe I just heard her wrong, "A what?" Oh my god. "Do demons eat people? I thought this was a soon-to-be-friendship..." I'm definitely taking a nap when I get home. If I get home...

Karma seemed to think for a minute. Apparently 'do you eat people' is a hard question to answer. Who knew? "It is. At least, I would like it to be. I'm not evil. I'm a normal person. I was raised by humans - like you - but when an asshole showed up at *my* front door, he told me I was a demon instead of an angel."

Michael technically didn't call me an angel until last night, but I don't think that matters right now. "So, yours is a jerk too?"

"Oh definitely." She laughed. Then, she leaned forward on the table so she could speak at a lower volume. That's probably a good idea. They're not overly busy right now, but they're busy enough for us to be cautious. "Are you really a Virtue? That's our theory, at least."

I tilted my head, "*Our*? Does your mentor actually talk to you about all this Heaven and Hell stuff? Michael doesn't think my *tiny human mind* could handle it." Not that he said those exact words, but he has no problem implying it. "All he told me was that there's an apocalypse coming, and that I have a roll to play in stopping it." I would *like* for him to tell me more, even if it's scary, but I can't even ask him since he hasn't been *home* in a week.

"Really? Roman is pretty open with this stuff." She paused, cursed, and ran her hand over her face. "Don't mention his name to Michael, please. Apparently they know each other."

"They do? Are they friends?" Can angels and demons be friends? Can Michael actually *make* friends? I pursed my lips, "Do archangels and whatever yours is have friends?"

Karma smirked, her eyes darting to the windows again, "According to Roman, they aren't friends. Imagine a fourteen year old boy talking about the kid that stole his first girlfriend."

I laughed at that. So Michael has a frenemy then. That's adorable. This must be the 'arch enemy' Michael was talking about. "I won't mention his name." Just then, May came back out with a tray. "I can see our food coming, but after we eat can we go somewhere without human ears and you can get me a little more up to speed? Would that be okay?"

Karma nodded, "Yeah! I'll do my best. Being in the dark about all this can't be fun." Understatement of the century. All I've learned is that there's much more to this than I've been told.

忍

"That was one of the best burgers I've ever had." Karma declared, rubbing her flat stomach.

I laughed at her antics, "I could tell. You ate all of yours *and* half of mine."

"You gave me permission." She reminded, bumping shoulders with me. I stumbled a bit, but I don't think she noticed. She's much stronger than she looks. "If you're ever in Monterey, I'll take you to *The Monument*. It's my favorite burger place back home. Though, warning, they're not steamed. I'd never had a steamed burger before." Ever? How crazy. Monterey must be where her house is. I wonder if it's anything like here.

Karma let me lead the way when we left the restaurant - and luckily was too focused on looking around to notice May teasing me on the way out. We were headed to the park Michael and I practiced magic in that first time. That seems like light years away now. Karma was still in a tank top, but didn't seem bothered by the fifty degree weather in the slightest. When we got to the park, Karma produced a camera with an expensive looking lens she screwed on after wiping off with a cloth.

"Wait," She grabbed my arm, effectively stopping me from moving. She approached the bench we were headed to with practiced stealth, and snapped some photos of one of the many little birds that lives here perched happily on the back of the bench. She was still snapping pictures as it flew away. "Beautiful." She murmured so quietly, I'm not sure she even heard it.

"You're a photographer?" I asked. A gust of wind blew past us, bringing a harsh chill with it. Karma didn't even notice. How strange.

She just shrugged, "Not a professional. It's just a hobby. This park is every photographer's dream. This whole place actually."

I shrugged, Telluride is a beautiful place, but I'm sure it pales in comparison to some other places. I sat of the bench, crossing my legs underneath me, "I grew up here, so it's hard to appreciate it the same way a tourist would. I've never been anywhere else. What about you? Did you grow up in Monterey?"

Karma sat beside me, dropping her arm over the back of the bench, ever so gracefully. For someone who looks so muscular and stocky, she was always so effortlessly graceful. I don't understand it. She sighed, "No. I moved to California when I was seventeen to finish high school at my grandmother's house. Then when I graduated, my grandmother signed over my mom's old house in Monterey to me so I could go to college there. I don't know where I was born exactly, but I was raised in Michigan." She tilted her head, frowning at whatever was in front of her, but I have a feeling it was an internal issue. "I guess I'm technically from Hell? I don't know if I was born there, though."

I shifted, turning my whole body to face her. She doesn't seem like someone who opens up easily, that deserves my full attention, "Do you miss it? Michigan?"

She let out a single dry laugh, like the mere thought was outrageous. Her eyes darkened as she glared off into space. I wouldn't be surprised if she forgot I was here.

"Karma?" She jumped, turning to face me with glossy eyes. I shouldn't of stayed silent so long, and I shouldn't have asked. That was a rabbit hole she was avoiding, and my nosiness threw her in. "Hey," I gently covered her hand with mine. Her skin was on fire, but I kept my hand there. "It's okay. I'm glad you got away from whatever was in Michigan." She still seemed lost. Her eyes wouldn't focus. "So," I pushed forward, "I have a few questions. If that's alright."

There we go. Her eyes finally refocused on mine, and she straightened. "Of course. I'll do my best to answer them."

I wrung my hands out, taking a steadying breath. I don't know if I'll get to see her again any time soon, so I should start with the important ones. "You're a demon, but you didn't know before you met your mentor?"

She nodded, "Yeah. I'm one of the Seven Sins, but I thought I was human - and was raised as one - until Roman showed up."

"One of the Seven Sins..." Seven Sins and Seven Virtues. That can't be a coincidence. "I'm one of the Seven Virtues. Do the Sins have specific qualities, too? For instance, I'm the Virtue of Patience."

She blinked, "Are you fucking serious?" What did I say wrong? "Sorry. I'm the Sin of Wrath." *Wrath is meant to be your weakness.* "I'm almost positive we're each other's opposite. We're probably not meant to be friends." Then she laughed, shaking her head.

"We seem to be okay," I giggled, gesturing to our hands in between us. "Is it just us? I haven't been told if there's any other Virtues, but I don't think Michael would tell me." He'd probably say it was just a distraction. "We're on a pretty need to know basis. Not by my choice."

She scoffed, "Doesn't the lack of answers drive you crazy?"

I shrugged, "Not really. I'm sure to a great celestial being, I do seem too small to understand things like this. He doesn't seem to spend much time around humans in general." Sometimes it's hard to remember that he's actually this powerful being that's literally the stuff of legends when he's yelling at me about grease, but that doesn't change what he is.

"You are patient," Karma snorted. She seemed almost amused by me. At least she's not counting. "We haven't found any other Sins. Yet. We're looking, though."

"Do you know what the other... Ah... Sins are?" What has happened to my life? "Michael said the other Virtues are Chastity, Temperance, Generosity, Diligence, Kindness, and Humility." I laughed, shaking my head at how ridiculous I sounded. "We sound like a church group. The kind that goes caroling on Christmas morning." I wonder if people actually do that.

"They do sound like a... Fun bunch." I gave her a flat look. That was the most blatant lie. You'd think demons could lie better. "According to Roman, the other Sins are Lust, Gluttony, Greed, Sloth, Envy, and Pride."

"So... A bar fight?" She smiled at me. "Are you sure you want to find the rest? One bad argument could get bad alarmingly fast." If it does happen, I hope it's not an argument that takes place around me.

Karma sighed, running a hand through her hair, pulling the ponytail out with it. "I think so. I mean, yours sound like an absolute bore, and mine sounds like tequila personified." I snorted, that's an insanely accurate description. "At the same time, they are the few people who will understand what it's like to be us. Plus, we can't save the world without them."

"Right." My shoulders sagged as I rested my head in my palms. "I don't know how I forgot about all that. It's all Michael and Yhwh seem to talk about."

"So you've met him, too? I've recently met Yhwh. He's... Not what I expected." She met Yhwh? Michael actually told him about her. So much for him not hurting my friends anymore. I guess he must really be like his father.

"You mean terrifying?" I shuddered, thinking back to Yhwh's eyes. "He's so *cold*. I never thought God would be so scary. When Michael said I was going to meet him, I was so excited. I'd thought Michael was just stressed - being in charge of God's army can't be easy, right?" Not to mention he's also training me. Hopefully God can't hear me calling him God after he told me not to.

"In reality, he's just like his father?" A part of me really hopes not.

"Yeah," I sighed, "Though, I don't suppose I can complain..." Michael could just stop teaching me and leave me to someone else. From the way Yhwh talked, the next person would definitely try to break me.

"Why not?" Karma's grip tightened on the bench, "Some *jackass* shows up on your front door, drops a crazy amount of responsibility on your shoulders, won't tell you a damn thing, introduces you to one of the scariest beings in the universe, and a truck load of other shit. You have every right to complain." I couldn't help laughing. Michael would absolutely hate Karma. She's so outspoken. It would drive him crazy.

"Well, yes, but you have Lucifer. Surely he's worse, and a lot scarier." He *is* Satan, after all. He's like the supreme evil.

Karma shrugged, watching a squirrel dart way too close to the bench, "I've only spoke to him once, but he wasn't like Yhwh. Yeah sure, he was scary and I couldn't really see any compassion in his eyes, but he was honest. With Yhwh, he looked at me like a pawn. Like some*thing* he could maneuver the way he wants and dispose of after." Yeah, I can definitely see how she got that impression. He even treats Michael that way. "Lucifer didn't want to play games, though. He doesn't want the world to end. He doesn't seem to care if I'm on his side or not as long as everyone survives. I don't really know *why* he wants the world to survive, but obviously he does."

"Lucifer is better than God? That's fantastic." Maybe I'm on the wrong side. "This whole thing is crazy."

"Definitely, and I don't think our "mentors" understand how much of a shock this can be for a person." Now, *that* is something I can fully agree with.

I stiffened, seeing an incredibly *large* man approaching us. He looked like seven bodybuilders smooshed into one person. "Um, is that Roman? He doesn't look like an actual human male." I'd never seen anyone so *big*. No wonder Michael hates him. He's several inches taller Michael and much wider... Maybe not with Michael's wings, but he doesn't have those when he's here.

Karma groaned, "Hang back. *Damn him*." Roman stopped when he saw Karma jogging to him angrily. In her haste, she forgot her camera, leaving it beside me. I picked it up carefully, and snapped a couple photos of myself with plenty of goofy faces. If I know anything about her, it's that she'd laugh when she saw them.

Across the park, Karma and Roman were arguing, standing closely together - I'm assuming to avoid anyone overhearing - or they just don't realize they're that close. Karma stuffed her hands into her back pockets. It wasn't a show of her being relaxed, though. It was definitely a way to hold herself back. Maybe I should go help.

"Karma?" I asked, coming up behind her. Karma pulled her hands out of her pockets to take her camera back, and put it in her own bag. "I should go. Michael gets angry if I disappear for too long." Michael isn't home so he probably wouldn't *know,* but I seem to be causing some issues with the two of them. That's the opposite of what I want to do. I'd hate for Karma to have problems because of me. Friends don't do that to each other.

Roman scoffed, crossing his arms across his chest. I thought Karma's arms were muscular... Jeez. Roman's arm was bigger than my head. "That is because he is a... What do humans say? Control freak." He nodded at the phrase, "And an *asshole*."

I snickered into my hand, "So you were right about that, huh?" Karma smirked, holding in her own laugh. She avoided Roman's eyes, still smiling.

"So when you said 'discussing sensitive information' you meant talking ill about me? How *mature* of you, Karma." Now Karma was full on laughing, which only made him glare harder. It wasn't even focused on me, and it made me nervous. Karma cared less about his glare than she cared about the cold weather. He rolled his eyes at her, and focused on me, "Hello. Medusa, correct?"

"Yeah," I laughed, "Hello. Is there a formal introduction I'm supposed to do? Medusa Sinclair, Virtue of Patience. It's nice to meet you." I smiled. Should I bow, or curtsey, or something?

Roman stopped glaring, and smiled softly at me, "That was exemplary. Karma could never be that polite." Karma flipped him off. He smirked at Karma, "How are you getting along with the Virtue of Patience? I would have thought simply being around her would put you on edge. Is that not the case?"

"*No, actually.*" Karma snarked back, "She's pretty calming. Oddly enough, we get along great. Maybe it's a yin and yang thing."

I think that's the nicest thing I've ever heard someone call me. I like the thought of being calming. "Opposites attract," I supplied, "Not all of the time though. Michael doesn't seem to like me all that much. The two of you get along much better than we ever could." They bicker a lot, but even I can tell they get along really well. The pair exchanged a glance before frowning at me. Perfectly in sync. I laughed again, "You have no idea how the two of you look right now. Arms all crossed, standing with your feet equally apart, frowning down at me." Karma shifted, dropping her arms. She looked over her male counterpart before rolling her eyes. She really didn't know how similar they looked. How funny. "You're adorable. Do you have something I can write my number on? So we don't lose contact."

"Yeah." Karma produced a receipt from her bag along with a pen, and handed them over. "Good luck with Michael." I beamed at her, and kissed Roman's cheek before heading back to my bike. He reminds me of a bulldog. All grumpy looking but really just wants a hug.

May was waiting outside *Steamie's* when I got back. A smile overtook her face when she saw me approaching, "Hey, gorgeous. Who was your friend?"

I gave her a flat look, unlocking my bike. "I don't like your tone. She's just a friend."

"A very attractive friend. What is it about you that attracts tall lesbians?"

I'm so happy she's having such a field day with this. Even if she's completely wrong. "I don't attract lesbians. I met my first lesbian *last night* with you. I don't even know if Karma likes women."

She huffed, "She should. With an ass and legs like that, I'd switch teams."

"You're terrible." I laughed, shaking my head at her, "Don't you have customers waiting on you?" She *is* still in her uniform.

"I'm on break, but I should head back. I'll text you later, yeah?" I nodded at her. It should be a quiet day when I get back home. At least, I hope so. May paused at the door, "Oh and if we're placing bets, my bet is totally on you and Karma. You vibe better. Michael is still sexy, though, so it's not like there's a losing option."

Chapter Eight

    I leaned my bike against the house, and headed inside. Dad was on the couch, drinking a beer, watching whatever is playing on the sports channel. He didn't even glance at me when I passed him, but what's new?
    I felt much better after talking to Karma. Minus the fact that she's spoken to Yhwh, which is *completely* my fault. If I hadn't held her back at the store, Michael would've never met her. I do wish I could apologize for that. She probably wouldn't let me, and it might make her more inclined to hit Michael, so it's probably best to leave it alone.
    Oh, darn! I meant to ask if she was struggling with her magic. She definitely has some form of it, if the silverware is anything to go by. Hopefully I'll get the chance to see her again before she goes back home.
    "There you are." I screamed, not expecting him to be there. Michael, now scowling, crossed his arms, "*Why* are you screaming?"
    "Why are you suddenly in my room?! You scared me half to death!" I slipped off my shoes, and climbed onto my bed. Michael stayed standing so he could have an optimal glaring angle. "You've been gone for days. Some warning would be nice."
    "How was I supposed to warn you? You're never *home*. You heard what my Father said, you need to be improving. Not going out with the mortals, or that ridiculous boy that keeps seeking you out." What is he even talking about? The only male I see

on a regular basis is Brian, and he does not seek me out. "Get changed out of that pink monstrosity. We're going to train."

I moved to get up, but paused. Maybe Michael does need someone like Karma. I moved back to a sitting position, square in the middle of my bed. *You have every right to complain*. And dang it, I have some things I really want to get off my chest. "No."

"*What* did you say?"

"I said, no. I don't want to train; I want to talk. So sit." I pointed to the opposite side of the bed.

"Medusa-"

"*No*. I'm sick of this, and I'm sick of being in the dark about everything. So sit down. We are going to talk like normal people. I *deserve* that." My hands shook as I glared back at Michael. He hadn't moved, but neither had I. I need to stand up for myself or I'm going to get stomped on. Maybe not by Michael himself, but I'm sure Yhwh can find someone to do it for him. "Be honest with me," I pleaded, "*Please*."

He growled, but took a seat on my bed. Michael sat fully facing me with his arms crossed, "I don't know what the hell has gotten into you, and I *do not* approve."

"Well, I'm sick of caring." Maybe not completely, but enough. I straightened my spine, refusing to acknowledge the chills running down it. Michael was making the room much colder than it was supposed to be, and my thin sweater wasn't doing much to protect me. But if I get up now, I lose this chance. "I have questions, and you need to answer them. You can't expect me to just keep following you blindly. Have you found any other

Virtues? Does anyone have an idea where they might be? What's the plan when we find them?"

Michael relaxed slightly, but was still scowling at me. Baby steps, I suppose. I was right, though. He'd really hate Karma. "No, no other Virtues have been located. I believe my father has some scouts in several places, but I do not know where. When they are found, they will be sent an Angel guardian to train them, as I am training you. Is that all?"

"Nope. Settle in, I'm just getting started. I want to be there. When the next Virtue is training, I want to be there with them. Going through this alone isn't something I would wish on anyone. I can help them."

Michael scoffed, "Help them? You can't even master your own magic. What help are you going to be to them?"

I will not cry. I balled up my fists to stop the tremors, "Stop it. Don't belittle me." That's all everyone has done my whole life. I don't need it from him too. Or Yhwh for that matter. "I want to be there to help the people going through what I'm going through." If they have a mentor like Michael, they're going to need me. It's impossible to succeed with people constantly knocking you back down. "The last thing Humility or Kindness needs is for someone like *you* to burst into their life and make them miserable."

"Someone like me?" He huffed, "Do you not realize how lucky you are to have me here? You are being trained by the greatest general of all time. I have trained many great soldiers-"

"But I'm *not* a soldier!" Why can't he *get* that?

"You need to be!" Great now we're both yelling. A vein was bulging in Michael's forehead as he yelled back at me, "This isn't some ridiculous game, Medusa! The world is coming to an end and you are in charge of stopping it. Do you think the apocalypse is going to cease because you bat your big green eyes and *ask* it to? Are you going to tear up like you're doing now and pray it works?"

I wasn't... Okay I was, but it was out of anger. I didn't know anger could make you cry, but I've learned a lot today. Michael watched me get up from my bed looking stupidly smug. He probably thought I had given in and was going to change. Well screw him. I slipped on my flats, and marched out the door.

"What the hell was all the yelling about?" I ignored my father on the way out the back door. What does he care? It's four o'clock in the afternoon, he's already too drunk to remember any of this anyway.

"Medusa, where are you going?" Michael ignored him as well, following me. "If you were going to leave, you went out the wrong door."

"Oh wow, Michael, thanks for telling me how to operate the house I've lived in for twenty three years. I still get lost in there sometimes. Thank God I have someone like you constantly telling me how stupid I am." Anger is exhausting, but that didn't make me any less angry.

"You are being irrational. What happened to the Medusa that was here when I left?"

I spun around, facing his scowl head on, "That's what happened! You left! You only came back to gripe at me, and then to whisk me away to meet the most terrifying being I have ever met, and then you left me alone to deal with that. God himself basically called me useless. Do you know what that does to a person?" I let out a dry laugh, "Actually, I'm sure you do know. You just don't care." That's the base of it, really. Karma and Roman showed me that, most likely without either of them realizing. Roman cared about Karma. He cared about where she was, they joke together and bicker one second later, they know each other so well that most of their conversations were spoken through glances and eye rolls. *That's* a good partnership. I'm just...

I'm just a pawn.

"Medu-"

"Brother, there you are." I turned to see some other tall man in my backyard. Well, angel, I suppose. This is the longest Tuesday ever. "Father said you might need my assistance with the Virtue. Is this her?"

"I do not need your assistance." Michael grumbled, moving himself in between his brother and me.

The new angel huffed, "Yes, I can see that by the way she is yelling at you. You made the Virtue of Patience yell at you."

What? I moved around Michael, forcing the air around us forward. Newcomer flew backwards, only stopping when he slammed into a tree. Michael raised a brow at me, "You've been practicing."

"As a matter of fact, no I have not." I turned my back to him, and sat by the brook. What kind of world is this where the *demons* are nicer than the angels? I should've asked Karma to kidnap me.

"*Have you lost your mind?*" New guy was back up, and angry. Michael can handle him.

"Jophiel, that is a mistake." Michael warned. Hopefully Jophiel listens to his much bigger brother. A giant wall of ice appeared next to me, pulling another scream from me. I turned to glare at him, but he wasn't looking at me. He was scowling at his brother, "I told you that it would be a mistake."

"Wait, did he *attack* me?" I guess that's fair. I did throw him into a tree.

"*Yes.*" Michael still didn't look at me. He kept his eyes trained on his brother.

"Why would you do that? Have you forgotten that she is a soldier? She needs to be able to take an attack!"

"No, I am not!" Michael grabbed my outstretched hand, and pulled me to my feet. The angel scowled at me - unfortunately it didn't have the desired effect since I've spent the last few months with the champion of glaring. "I am *not* a soldier."

His golden eyes focused firmly on me, "Then you are useless."

I am so sick of men telling me how useless I am. "Did it ever occur to you that you can stop someone from being the Virtue of Patience by driving her insane? You're all really good at it."

"Translation; you are making it worse." Michael gave him a cold smile, "Time for you to go."

Jophiel shook his head, "Father will not approve of you sending me away."

"He wouldn't approve of me killing you either." Michael shot back. Why is he so okay with murder? "Now, Medusa has done enough for today. How about a nap, Medusa?"

"That sounds fantastic." I nodded, heading back into the house. So much for calming down outside. Stupid angels.

"Oh, and brother," Michael called, walking beside me, "You attack Medusa and you attack me. Whether the two of us were arguing or not. I suggest you remember that."

We made it back to my room in silence. Dad was asleep when we went though the living room. How did he fall asleep so fast? I paused to turn off the television before continuing to my room. Electric is expensive enough. Michael leaned on my closed door, watching me move around my room.

"Have you ever heard the word creepy, Michael?" I asked, moving into my closet.

"Once or twice I suppose. I know what it means, if that is what you are asking. Are you done being angry at me already?" He didn't follow me into the closet - thankfully. I guess he finally learned *that* lesson.

"I don't know." I shrugged, "I was mad and I'm still angry about things, but I'm tired. I'm just *so* tired. Anger is exhausting."

"Especially for you, I'd imagine. As I've previously stated, Wrath is your weakness. Being too angry could have a series of negative effects on you. How are you feeling?"

"Fine. I feel fine." Just tired. It's been a long day. I came out of the closet fully dressed in pajamas.

Michael frowned at me, "I have seen you wear the same t-shirt no less than thirteen times, but have never seen you wear the same set of pajamas twice. Why do you have so many?"

"I like pajamas." I shrugged, settling into my bed with my smaller pillow in my lap. "Why do you always wear really tight shirts?"

He pulled his shirt away from his chest, "Is this not normal?"

"Not really, but it looks nice on you. Are you going to sit down?" I tilted my head at him. Michael sighed, moving to sit on the bed beside me. "I'm sorry I yelled at you."

"It was well deserved on my part. I do believe in you, Medusa. You've gotten so much stronger since we started training. I apologize for what my father and my brothers have said about you. I do not believe that you are useless. However," He held up a finger, "I do agree that you are not a soldier. Not in the slightest." He chuckled.

"Okay, okay." I laughed, leaning my head on his shoulder. "I could still be of use to the other Virtues, though." If Karma is correct, maybe I can help them feel a little less stressed with my 'calming' affect.

"I do believe that. I will tell my Father that we need to be the ones to train the next Virtue, and I vow to not make you angry this time. How was the transport for you? I was careful to hold onto you when I took you to Zion. Did you handle the trip back alright?"

"No," I scoffed, "I threw up for about two hours, and I might have a minor concussion from hitting the frame of my bed."

"What? Why didn't you say something? What spot?" He bumped me off his arm, making me sit up. I showed him the spot that I hit. "I can fix this." That makes me nervous. Michael rubbed the spot on my head leaving a cool sensation in his wake. I couldn't help leaning into his touch. My head did feel much better. "You did have a concussion. I apologize for not checking on you sooner." I didn't think he would ever apologize this much.

"Thank you, Michael. Do you think, that maybe, we can try to be honest with each other from here forward? I'd like to be friends."

"I don't really have friends, Medusa, so I cannot promise that I will be any good at it, but I will try to be easier to work with. Now, you get some rest." He rubbed my back, "I will come and get you in a few hours."

忍

My eyes fluttered open, immediately shutting once more. Did Michael open my curtains again? I thought we'd come so far. I pulled my blanket over my head, well, I tried to anyway. I ended up just dumping grass all over my face. Now I'm awake.

"Michael!" I groaned, wiping the dirt off my face. Why would he do this? "Michael?" I blinked. I was alone in a massive field. I clambered to my feet, brushing the grass off of me. There wasn't anything for miles. Just grass and wild flowers. So many flowers, holy crap. It definitely isn't Telluride, that's for sure.

"*Ciao c'è qualcuno?*"

He left me with people? What kind of training exercise is this? And why is it *so hot* here?

"*Ti sei perso?*" A woman slightly taller than me with her hands clasped in front of her approached me. Her light brown eyes were filled with concern, "*Parli Italiano?*"

"Um," I glanced around. Where had she come from? "English? Sorry I don't speak... Italian?" I think that's what she's speaking.

"*Oh! Americano?*"

"Yes!" Now if I can figure out where we *are*. I guess Michael couldn't drop me off with my phone. That would be too easy. I turned back to the woman, "Do you know where we are?" She gave me a pained smile. She can't understand me. Dang it, I should've taken Italian in high school instead of French.

"*Da dove vieni?*" I guess she understands my frustration with this. Though, judging by her lack of pockets, I'm assuming she doesn't have a phone either. "*Ah, no Italiano.*" She wrung her hands out, "*Mi chiamo Jez. Vieni con me?*"

She held her hand out to me, trying to wave me along. "Oh, no, I should stay here." Hopefully Michael will come and grab me soon. What did he expect to happen when he left me out here?

The woman frowned, "*No no, vein con me.*" Well at least I think I learned a little Italian from this. She's definitely trying to get me to go with her somewhere. Is there a better patch of flowers than this one?

"Medusa."

I whipped around, "Michael! Michael?" There was no one there. It was still just me and this woman.

"*Con chi stai parlando? Siamo solo noi qui fuori.*"

I ignored her, looking around for him. "Medusa, come on." Come on where? "Medusa!"

I gasped feeling a hard tug on my chest. I was pulled from the field... And sat up in my bed. Michael was sitting next to me, violently shaking me awake. "Okay okay. I'm awake. Please stop doing that." That was a dream? It felt so real.

"What happened? Your magic aura was more active than I had seen... Well, ever. Are you alright?" What is a magic aura?

"I'm okay. Can magic give weird dreams?"

"I don't dream, and as far as I know, they can not trigger dreams. What kind of dream was it? My father can travel through dreams, but he has other ways to reach you." That's creepy, but what else is new when it comes to Yhwh?

"I was in a beautiful field surrounded by wildflowers... There was a girl there. She kept talking me, but not in a language I know. I only know English and *very* basic French, so that doesn't leave much room, but still."

Michael nodded, staying quiet. He thought for a moment. Well, I think he's thinking. Hopefully he's not counting. I pulled my hair back into a bun while I waited. Michael refocused on me, "Can you attempt to repeat something she said to you?" Oh dear. I tried to repeat her 'come with me' sentence she kept saying. Michael flinched at my butchering of the language, but nodded nonetheless. "I believe the original language is meant to be Italian. Any other details about this woman?"

"She's very conservative? Lots of hair?" I shrugged.

Michael frowned at me, "That isn't helpful. Anything near by?"

"Lots of flowers, and a giant hill that looked to have a little church. Maybe a town?"

He nodded, seeming to think it over. "A church? That could be helpful. Did it look like she was part of the church? A nun, perhaps?"

"A nun? Why would you *want* me to dream about a nun?"

He gave me a flat look, "Nuns devote their lives to my father. Do you know who else is most likely to devote themselves to Yhwh?" People that haven't met him? *"Virtues."* Oh. *"*Exactly. There's a chance you're connected with this person because she's another Virtue. Your magic could be on the same... Um..."

"Wavelength." I finished. I hadn't even considered that. Could I really be connected to the other Virtues? "I don't think you're going to have a strong team, Michael. I didn't learn much about her though the large language barrier, but she seemed to be similar to me in terms of physical strength. She's a little taller, but she was out there with a basket of flowers."

Michael just sighed, "Your magic can be your strength once we figure out how to truly harness it. As for the girl... Well, let's wait and see if she comes up as a Virtue at all before we do that." Yeah, best not to stress about a possibility. For all we know, it could've been some magic induced dream with no base in reality. "I will need to update my father, though. He can have some of his scouts focus on Italy."

"Wait," Michael got up to leave, but paused, "I still want to be the ones to mentor her."

He gave me a single nod, "I will make sure we are the ones to go meet her. I give you my word." The word of an angel? Hopefully it means something.

Once he was gone, I climbed out of bed, and made my way downstairs. Dad was no where to be seen. He must have relocated to his room before crashing again. I made my way to the fridge to see if we had anything. I should've really gone grocery shopping after lunch.

"Oh," Did I forget that I went grocery shopping? Surely, I wouldn't forget something like that. At least I hope I wouldn't. Dad doesn't leave the house, and I seriously doubt he knows about grocery delivery. Even if he did, he would never buy this much fruit. Or kale. *Oh my god.* Michael got groceries. He even bought a stand with little baskets to hold the apples, oranges, avocados, lemons, sweet potatoes, mushrooms, garlic, ginger, and more things that I've never even seen before. I do know one thing, he certainly didn't buy any bacon, beer, or red meat. He really is sticking to this no hamburger rule. "I guess it's a good thing I actually like fruits." We're going to have to talk about the lack of bread though. That's too far.

When Michael got back, he found me at the table eating a plate full of sliced fruits. He actually smiled at me. That's all it took? "Look at you." He took the seat beside me, still smiling. Then, he frowned. That didn't take long, "Why are there no vegetables on your plate? You need to have balance."

"It's a snack. Not a meal." I resisted sticking my tongue out at him. "You know what I do need?"

"If you say burgers, I'm making you try Muai Thai again." He threatened.

"*Bread.*" I'm never trying martial arts ever again, either. That was brutal. "You didn't buy any bread. Do you know who doesn't have bread in their house?"

"People who care about their health."

"Serial killers. They might be healthy, but they're definitely crazy. Plus, you got that turkey breast, and the lettuce. I could make such a good *healthy* sandwich." Healthy enough anyway. He doesn't have to know I'm going to put chipotle mayonnaise on it. Oh my god, did he throw out my chipotle mayonnaise?

He rolled his eyes at me, "You know, I have seen that people make these things called 'lettuce wraps' it's like a sandwich, but instead of bread they use lettuce. You should try that."

"*Or* I buy bread and don't get hamburger meat or sodas. Oh, and you have to deal with my dad when he finds out you didn't get any of the foods he actually likes." That is definitely not something I want to deal with.

"The only person more unhealthy than you, is Elias. Some healthy eating could do him some good, and *sunlight*." He sneered at the television in the next room. I wish him luck with that. That tv has been his constant companion since Mom died. He watched me for a moment before pushing his chair away from the table, "I'm going to make you something with more nutrients."

"No! That is not necessary. This is enough for me." He scowled at me, eyes flicking between my plate and my face. He obviously didn't believe me, but I'd rather starve that have to suffer through that burrito again. My stomach churned just thinking about it.

"You need *sustenance*, Medusa. I am making you an actual breakfast. What do you want in your omelet?" Omelet? That doesn't sound bad. Plus, he's actually asking me.

"Eggs, cheese, onion, and the red bell peppers. No avocados. Absolutely zero." I can't. Michael rolled his eyes at me, but I didn't see him grab any when he gathered his ingredients. Though, I'm sure that it's possible he snuck some.

Michael was still cooking when my father hobbled into the kitchen some minutes later. Here we go. He made his way to the fridge and peered in. Glasses clinked as he shoved things around the items in the fridge. Michael spoke up when he started moving the plastic bags, "Those are delicate. Don't break or bruise them, Elias."

My father ignored him, "Where the hell is the beer?" He straightened to glare at me over the fridge door, "Did you forget to buy beer?"

"No," Michael answered, transferring the omelet to a plate. It actually looked pretty good. "I purposefully didn't grab the beer. Alcoholism can cause memory loss, affect your coordination negatively, weaken your heart, break down your liver, lead to fat gather in your liver, cause liver failure, cause pancreatitis, and several other complications. You need to stop drinking it."

My father whipped around, his face already turning red. He got in Michael's face - to the best of his ability. Michael has nearly a foot on him in height, pointing a finger at him, "Listen, *boy,* you don't tell me what to do. Now go get me some *damn beer!*"

Michael scowled, slowly moving my father's hand away from his face. Frost gathered on the stainless steel of the refrigerator as Michael glared back, "No." My father turned to me, "Don't yell at her either. She isn't bringing any alcohol in this house, just as I am not." I shrugged at my father. There's nothing I could do. Michael is much more terrifying than my father could ever be.

Michael crossed to the table, setting the omelet down in front of me, "Elias, there is food in the kitchen that will not kill you. If you are thirsty, there is water and natural fruit juices."

My father glared at him. He moved around the kitchen while I ate my omelet. Michael ignored him in favor of watching me eat. Maybe I should go help him. I was on my last bite of the omelet - which was much more delicious than I dared to hope it would be - my father had another outburst, "Where is the bacon?"

"In Hell where it belongs." Michael deadpanned, still not turning around. I coughed to cover up my laugh. My father didn't appreciate either of our responses.

"Do you want me to make you something, Dad?"

Before he could answer, Michael cut in, "No time. Your father is a grown man. We have things to do." We have more things to do? He got up, waving me along. I pulled myself from my chair, opting to follow Michael then suffer through another explosion from my father.

I jogged to catch up to Michael as he made his way out back. How does he walk *so* fast? I was slightly out of breath when I caught him, but I did catch up. "So," I stopped, putting my hands on my knees. Okay, maybe more than a little out of breath...

"You're horribly out of shape." He commented, stopping a few feet in front of me.

"Thanks. I have a question." I dropped onto the soft grass, crossing my legs. Michael scowled, but waved me to go on. I guess he isn't sitting with me. Not that I can be all that surprised. "What is a magic aura? It's been bugging me since you said it." And if there's one thing I've learned from him, it's that if I don't ask he'll never tell me.

"Do you know what an aura is?" I nodded. Michael moved closer to me, but remained standing. "Humans came close to understanding what an aura actually is, of course they never *fully* understood it as they refuse to believe in magic. However, the belief that your aura is an essential part of who you are and reflecting your spirit are actually correct. All humans have magic inside them, some just have less than others. You can tell how much magic someone has by seeing how vibrant their aura is, or the color of it." That's... interesting. "For example, your aura closely resembles that of an angel. If another angel were to see your aura, they would assume you are one of us without question. Until you spoke, that is." He shrugged, "When I woke you up, your body was covered in your aura, and was so bright I could barely see your body *or* your bed. I've never seen anything like it." I don't think he meant for that to be as scary as it sounded. Surely, it was just because that girl is a Virtue. If the scouts come back and say that she isn't, then I can have a minor nervous breakdown at being turned into a star. Simple.

"So if my aura looks like an angel, what do normal people's look like? Like my father."

His face twisted. Michael looked toward the house as if he could scowl at my father through a wall and a wooden door, "Your father does not have a normal aura either, Medusa." That doesn't sound good. Is it because he lives with me? Or because I'm his daughter? "Elias' aura is filled with browns, blacks, and purples. His soul is filled with sin and sadness." Michael settled into the ground in front of me, clasping his hands in front of himself. "If you were to see your father's aura, your female friend from the park's aura, and your boss' aura side by side you would see a distinct difference in colors." I guess that makes sense. They're all very different people. "Starting with your boss…"

"Brian." I filled in.

He nodded, "Brian's aura is a mixture of light grey, vibrant pinks, and royal blues - all of which are positive things. Mainly meaning that he's content with his current situation in life and is a generous person. However, he also has a silvery blue mixed in with his aura which is a side effect of spending time with you. Your father who lives with you and has for your entire life, *should* have that on his aura as well."

I shifted. A chill made its way up my spine as he stared impassively at me. Something tells me I'm not going to like the answer to this question. I drew in a deep breath, "What does it mean if he doesn't have any traces of me?"

Michael sighed, "It means that his soul is overpowering any affect yours could have on him." My soul can have an effect on someone else's? If I can make other people more patient, Brian is going to strangle me. "Stop making that face. It really isn't that surprising considering how long his addiction has run rampant."

I pursed my lips, looking away from him. Michael didn't seem to notice, not that I really expected him to. He's becoming less like a living Brillo pad, but not that much. "Are you crying?" I shook my head. Michael scoffed, "Well, at least you're a terrible liar."

"Is it time for me to go to work yet?"

"It's still Tuesday." I groaned, flopping on my back. This day is the longest day in history.

Michael leaned over me with a brow raised, "Do you want dinner?"

I laughed, "I just ate." I don't really eat that much. Michael just shrugged. "I want to go to bed and not have a confusing dream." Oh, and for my magic aura to not go crazy. I didn't feel it, but I definitely don't like it.

"Then stretch and we'll go to bed." Stretch? I glanced at him, not moving. He gave me a flat look, "It will relax you, so hopefully you'll go into a deep sleep easier. Unless you want to try an actual work out to tire you out?"

"Stop threatening me." I grumbled halfheartedly. Michael smirked, rising to his feet as well. "Know any good stretches that won't put me in pain?"

"I guess we'll find out."

忍

My phone rang, startling me awake. I snatched it off my bedside table, glancing at the clock. Who in their right mind is calling me at three in the morning? Oh, it's Karma.

"Karma?" I paused to yawn, "It's three in morning..."

"I know. I'm sorry. I just..." She sounds so defeated. I didn't think she could be defeated.

Feeling more awake, I sat up in my bed. I have no idea where Michael wondered off to, but I'm glad he did. He'd give me the lecture of a lifetime if he found out I was talking to her after deeming her 'suspicious' or whatever word he used. "It's okay. What's up?" I couldn't hold back the second yawn.

Karma sighed, "Michael and Yhwh are close, right?"

"Yeah." Weird direction of conversation. Then again, nothing is really normal at three in the morning anyway. "I think so. Why?"

"I just spoke to him." *What?* "Yhwh, not Michael. Be careful around them, okay? Yhwh said some things that make me really uncomfortable. I'm not so sure about my side of things either, but I know for sure there is something wrong with Yhwh."

That doesn't sound good at all. "Okay, I will be careful." I promised, "Karma, is everything okay? You're worrying me." Chills made their way down my spine in a never ending loop. Something was *seriously* wrong. I don't know how I know, but there's not a doubt in my mind that she isn't okay. "What's the matter? Be honest."

Karma let out a frustrated sigh, growling slightly, "He brought up the worst parts of my past, and shrugged them off like they were nothing. There are a lot of things in my past that are living nightmares. *Nightmares.* He looked me in the eye and told me they weren't that bad. He said he couldn't condemn my..." She paused, almost choking on her next words. If it was anyone else, I'd think she was feeling depressed with the whole situation, but this is Karma, the Sin of *Wrath*. She's *angry,* and Yhwh is making it worse. "Assailant for what he did." She finished, "*Anyone* who says that about what I went through..."

"Is heartless." I finished for her. I ran my hands through my hair, wishing I had something, anything, to say that could make her feel better. "I don't know what you went through - which is fine; you don't have to talk about it - and I will be extra careful. Maybe add an extra extra in that. Thank you for the warning." I sighed, "I wish I could do the same. They don't tell me anything. They just boss me around." I would love to give her some form of advice or information that could be a leg up, but I just didn't have any to give.

"Just focus on being there for the other Virtues. Judging from our experiences, they're going to need it. I think if we can trust each other, it doesn't matter what Lucifer and Yhwh are doing. I'm sorry for waking you up. I'll let you go back to sleep."

I smiled, despite her not being able to see me, "It's *more* than okay. You can wake me up at anytime." I laughed, "I agree, though. As long as we're united with each other, it doesn't matter what those trigger happy gods are up to. Goodnight, Karma. Try to get some actual rest, okay?"

She laughed, "I'll do my best. Goodnight, and *be safe.*"

Aye, aye Captain. I settled back into my bed. I hope Karma is alright. Wherever she is.

Chapter Nine

"Honey, I'm home!" Where is he? I didn't see Brian when I crossed through the store, the entire front was a ghost town. That's strange. I made it into the break room and found him sitting at the table with his arms folded. "Brian? Are you okay?"

"Hmm?" He blinked, turning his head slightly, but not enough to look at me. "Hey, Medusa. You're early again."

"Benefits of Michael being so on top of things," I shrugged, "You okay? I didn't see anyone at the front." I clocked in, keeping him in my peripheral vision. He seemed so down. It was bizarre.

"Oh they're up there. Nitpicking everything, I'm sure." He sighed, deflating into his chair.

"Who?"

"The shelving could be straighter, and we saw an entire basket of un-shelved items by the front counter." An older couple burst into the room, frowns firmly etched in their faces. The woman had designer glasses perched on the top of her blonde hair, and one of the tightest pencil dresses I have ever seen paired with sky high pointed toe heels. The man was dressed in a crisp button up and black slacks. All in all not unusual for visitors in Telluride, but it *is* unusual for the break room. The woman gave me a once over, "Who is this?"

Brian sighed again, rising to his feet. He stood next to me with his hands in his pockets, "Mother, Father, this is Medusa. She is our best employee and has been for the past six years." *Oh.* These are his parents? They don't look anything like him. Maybe the eye shape is the same? I guess. "Medusa, you can go ahead and man the store."

"Empty the cart by the front." Mrs. Whittle snapped as I passed her.

"No," Brian all but growled, "Medusa stick to the normal way we do things. Mom, you can't do that. You'll mess up-" I was gone before he finished.

He doesn't need me butting in on his family drama. Brian has always respected my personal space when it comes to personal issues. It's only human to give him the same curtesy. Plus, I've never minded working the store alone. Now that the holiday season is picking up, we'll have to have more people working at a time to handle the influx of people. Right now, though, it was nice and cal-

"There you are, Patience." The angel I threw into the tree yesterday waltzed into the store, and up to the counter. "We have things we need to discuss without my brother hovering."

"My name is Medusa. Just like yours is Jophiel, correct?"

He nodded, once. His eyes scanned the empty store, "Patience is your Heavenly name. You should want it to be spoken."

"I do not, and I would like for you to respect that." I replied, folding my hands together on the counter. This one talks more than Adakiel did, and now I'm not sure if that's a good thing.

The angel scoffed, "There is a *point* to this conversation, Patience." So there goes that, I guess. "Now to discuss my assisting you. I know my brother has been teaching you fighting styles and *trying* to hone your magical abilities." He straightened his shoulders, "I am here to teach you how to present yourself as the Heavenly being you are."

"Presenting myself to *whom* exactly?" I whispered, pausing to welcome the people coming into the store. "And do we have to do this here?" There are people here.

"Yes." He sneered at the family walking past. The father of the group scowled back at the angel. Jophiel rolled his eyes, refocusing on me. "Ignore the humans. They're irrelevant. You have plenty of people you need to worry about. Starting with my father, my brothers, and the remaining Virtues. The way they see you is imperative to how they view you as a leader."

"A leader?" Is that what I'm supposed to be to them? I was thinking more of a guide, and a friend. Maybe a mentor if they're up for that, but I don't want to be a *boss* to them.

Jophiel scowled at me, "Of course. Who else is meant to lead them? *Michael*?" He laughed dryly. "My brother cannot do that. Just as he showed he cannot even mentor you properly."

"Michael is doing a fantastic job as my mentor. Move please, I have actual customers." He scowled at the people as they passed him. I focused all of my attention on the customers as I checked them out, and sent them on their merry way. Such a happy group of people. They must be thrilled they beat the holiday rush for their vacation.

Before Jophiel had the chance to move back to lecture me or whatever he was here to do, Brian and his parents were moving to the front. His mother scowled, "The basket is still full. Do you *do* anything besides standing there like some kind of Barbie robot?"

"Do you know who you are *speaking to?*"

"Jophiel, these are my bosses." I interrupted, "Sorry about him. He's a little protective." I beamed, twisting my hands in front of me.

The only one not agitated was Brian, well I'm assuming he's not agitated with me. "Another brother, I presume?"

I giggled, biting into my lip. Brian's father glanced between the two of us, "Brian you are not fraternizing with one of our employees, are you?"

His mother hummed, "Well, I don't know if that's such a bad thing. She's cute. In a mousy way. Brian's honey brown hair, this girl's big green eyes that would be a perfect looking grandbaby to show off. I approve." Then she was gone with her husband trailing behind.

Brian rolled his eyes, "Ignore her, Medusa, and Michael's brother. I have no problem with the M and M wedding."

"Michael and I are not getting married any time soon." Let's not start *that* rumor. Michael didn't like the boyfriend thing starting, now we're talking about a *wedding*. Oh lord.

"Ah," Brian nodded, "Haven't asked your dad yet? What does he think of your Yeti, anyway?"

I glanced at Jophiel under the guise of not saying something in front of Michael's brother. Jophiel took it as an invitation, though, "Does your father disapprove of the work you and Michael are doing?"

"*Work.*" Brian scoffed, taking the basket his mother was so worried about. He got to work in the farthest aisle possible. So subtle that guy.

"So," Jophiel made his way back to me. He crossed his arms tightly across his chest as he glared at me in a poor attempt to mimic his older brother. He probably didn't see it that way, but that's how it looked to me. And unless he can read minds, he'll never know... Can angels read minds?! "Your father disapproves of our work?"

"No. He also doesn't *know* what Michael and I are doing. He thinks we're dating. It's a whole thing. Just don't interfere, okay?" This is exactly what I was afraid of. Angels invading my quiet hometown, and messing with the humans that live here. Michael is easy to nod at and ignore, because he's likely already ignoring them. But this guy? He tried to talk about who I was - *what* I am - to my bosses!

He made a noise, and nodded, "Patience." Then he was gone, leaving a single white feather in his place.

"Oh god." I darted around the counter to get the feather. The entire front of our store is windows! Someone could've seen him do that! "I definitely prefer Michael."

"That is good news." A laughing reply came from behind me. I dropped my head onto the counter top, ignoring the thud it made. I could feel the chill spread over the counter as Michael came to stand in front of me. "What is the matter? You seem worn out."

"A little." I finally picked my head up to look at the giant. Michael glanced around, "Brian is in the back of the store, if that's who you're looking for."

He scoffed, "I have never looked for Brian. No customers today?"

"Calm before the storm. People are going to start flocking to Telluride soon for their winter vacations. This is a ski town, you know?" He pinched the bridge of his nose, releasing possibly the longest sigh I have ever heard.

Brian actually made it back to the front before Michael was done sighing. He glanced at Michael before gesturing to him. I just shrugged. A good five minutes later, Michael's sigh tapered off, "I hate this town."

Brian laughed, "I hear that...Ahem." He coughed when he caught Michael's eye, "Sir. I met your brother, Michael. Lot more talkative than the last one."

"That isn't always a good thing." He is definitely correct about that. I never thought I'd agree with him so much. The last thing I need is Jophiel coming back here and telling Brian everything about me. "Did he irritate you, Medusa? I wasn't aware he was coming to see you today."

Oh no. That's bad. Michael seemed to have it controlled, but his eyes had frozen over, and his hands were balled into fists. He's going to *lose* it. Probably not near me, but it'll happen. At least, I hope it isn't near me.

"I'm fine, Michael. Why did you stop by?" He wasn't supposed to be here either.

"I wanted to check on you, and make sure you're doing alright. I know your health was called into question after your nap."

"I'm alright. Thank you for checking on me."

"That's my job." He tilted my chin up to kiss my cheek. "I'll see you when you get off."

When he was out of the store, and out of sight from all of the windows, Brian shook his head. He's going to get whiplash. "You two are the strangest couple."

忍

Michael waltzed into the store hours later, two minutes before I was set to clock out. "Your timing is amazing." He smirked at me, taking up his spot leaning on the counter. "You know, it's rare for me to leave work on time, right?"

"I know it's more likely you'll leave on time if I am here." That fair, I suppose. Though, I don't think scaring my boss is a good way to go about it.

"Hey, Misery." Amita bounded into the store, loudly smacking her gum. She did a double take when she spotted Michael leaning on the counter, "Oooh, and *who* are you, Adonis?"

Michael frowned, "My name is Michael. Do not compare me to the *Greeks*." He spat the word. He hates the Greeks? Surely he knows where my name comes from, right?

"Uh huh," She continued smacking, still looking him over. I doubt she heard anything he said, honestly. "Surely you don't want to be in this dump. Did'ya come to see me, *Michael*?"

"Go clock out so we can go home."

"Yes, sir." I saluted him as I passed. He didn't appreciate my 'good luck' as I went, though. Amita continued to loudly chew her gum while she attempted to flirt with the angel. Hopefully he isn't too mean to her.

Brian was in the break room when I entered. His head shot up, "No! No. Don't leave me with her."

I laughed, clocking out as dramatically as possible. "I think it's only fair since you abandon me with Mac constantly."

He scoffed, pushing himself up from the table. Brian met me at the door, "I always try to schedule us on the same days, because you're my favorite person to work with. You're my prized employee. And, like, my best friend."

"Fine," I gnawed on my bottom lip, trying to hide my smirk. "But Michael is waiting for me at the front, so if you want me to stay *you* have to tell him."

"Dammit. Damn boyfriend that benchpresses fucking trucks. Go have fun cuddling on the couch with Michael and a kale salad or whatever it is that you two do when you're alone. Don't tell me. That isn't information I need."

"I didn't *plan* on telling you what we do when we're alone, but I can tell you that if we're doing any cuddling and he grabs *kale;* that will be the ending to the cuddling." I'd also never cuddle with a glacier when stuffed animals exist, but Brian didn't know that. I bounded back to the front to find Michael glaring at the much smaller girl who was still popping her gum at him.

"Medusa! Are you ready to go?" I nodded at him, not caring to hide my smile. He nodded, gruffly pushing past Amita, "Goodbye, person I didn't care to learn the name of. Learn how to chew with your mouth closed. You are not *an infant.*" Amita gasped dramatically. Michael didn't slow his exit from the store.

"Amita! What did I say about gum?" *Uh oh.* Judging from that tone, she was definitely getting written up again. What does that put her at now? Surely, it's getting close to double digits.

"Brian can get angry?" Michael asked, leading me to the car.

"Oh, very." I'm not the one that normally sees it, since I prefer not to irritate the person who decides how many bills I can pay. From what I've heard, though, he can be pretty scary when he wants to be. "So, where are we going?"

"Your house," He scoffed, "We cannot train in that horribly colored shirt." What's wrong with orange? I thought it was a nice color. "After that, I have some ideas for how to further your magical abilities." Hopefully it's nicer than our other attempts at Michael's ideas.

We pulled up to the house moments later. The street was silent, almost eerily so, and a slight chill had settled over the silent town. It looks like we'll be getting snow soon. That should be fun. I wonder if I can get Michael to build a snowman with me. I bet with ice magic, we could build something amazing.

"Hey, Michael?" He hummed behind me, seemingly scanning the front yard. Is he ever relaxed? "How do you feel about snowmen?"

"I don't know what that is, so I don't have any particular feelings about them." He was still scanning when we entered the living room. "Where's Elias? This house is suspiciously quiet, don't you think?"

"I dunno," I shrugged, "Maybe he's showering?"

"Do you hear your loud water system? I don't." Okay, that was a fair point.

I pursed my lips, "Okay. Now you freaked me out. I'll go check his room. He's probably napping or something." I'm sure it's nothing. Who knows, maybe he actually wanted to get out of the house. That would be nice. Maybe he's taking the first step to fixing his aura.

Michael followed me to my father's room. This is where him constantly being on edge is a bad thing. I'm sure there's nothing to worry about, but the super general is on red alert. Surely that has to be exhausting. I pushed open my father's door with practiced silence - he can be extremely angry when he's woken up randomly. His bed was empty - a mess, but empty. "Dad?"

Michael pushed in the door further. He scanned the room before pointing, "His blanket is falling on that side. Perhaps he has started to fall off his bed in a similar manner that you do."

"I've only done that twice." But he did have a point. I moved to my dad's bed, stepping over all the random trash he had on the floor. How did he get this much stuff in here? I guess it *has* been a minute since I've cleaned it.

"You have done it several times. I found you on the floor just the other morning."

That isn't even slightly- "Oh my god! Dad?!" He was laying face down on the floor in a giant red circle. A dark red circle that had seeped so far into the carpet it wasn't even wet anymore.

"Medusa, get back." How can he say that? I can't just leave him here. I can't. I just... "Medusa. I need to analyze his wound so that we can find out what happened."

"What wound? I don't see an- Oh." What is with me? How could I miss the gaping hole in his back? Why is everything so blurry all of the sudden?

"Medusa. You are seconds away from hyperventilating. You need to step back, leave the room, and *breathe*." He hauled me to my feet, and away from my father. I protested as he dragged me to the door. He completely ignored me, though, and slammed the door in my face.

"Michael! Michael, please! Let me back in!" I hit the obnoxious door, not caring about the paint I was chipping or the red streaks that were appearing. I just... I need to be in there. "*Michael!*"

"Yelling does not equal breathing." Michael sighed, opening the door. I darted forward, rushing past him. My father wasn't on the floor anymore. He was on his freshly made bed with his hands folded on his stomach. "The stain in the carpet is gone as well. I thought this would make it easier for you to say goodbye."

I coughed, feeling my throat burn. Michael didn't speak as I sat beside my father on the bed. He didn't speak when my vision blurred so much I couldn't see the difference between my father's bo- body and his bed. Oh god. He's so cold. I can't remember ever being this close to him. After mom, he never wanted to be too close to me. I forgot about his laugh lines around his mouth, and that scar he has by his right eye. He always said it was from a fist fight, but Mom had written about him running into a wall the day he met her. She had to take him to the hospital. He said he was so distracted by her radiance that he stopped watching where he was going. He always called her his Angel for saving him that day. I thought it was a sweet story. I just wish they would've been able to tell it to me, instead of leaving it in a journal in the basement.

"You know, I don't remember my mom that well. I was so little when she died that it's hard to even picture her face some days." I cleared my throat. I don't even know if Michael is even in the room anymore. "But I remember when I was little, I would watch my parents cook together. They made a night of it, twice a week. They'd clear their schedules every Tuesday and Friday, and they'd spend hours cooking and playing around in the kitchen. They were *so* happy. And weekends they'd find some new recipe from the library or something and they'd perfect their method of making it. I'd just sit at the dining room table and watch them chop vegetables with giant smiles on their faces. I never understood it, but what all does a four year old understand? They acted like a night shut in the house chopping vegetables, making a roux, or having pots boil over on the stove was the perfect day.

"Then she was gone, and so were those days. I remember bringing him all her cookbooks every Tuesday and Friday after she died. He always ignored me. Until one day I came home, and he was standing over the grill. I thought he was *finally* cooking again. That I was finally waking him up. But when I went out there, I found ashes. He'd burned all of the cookbooks. Even Mom's favorites. She had this one, it was massive. I'll never forget the look of that thing. Wide spine with a blue and white checkered pattern, and some strange little macaron cartoons and their cake house. He said he burned that one first."

I don't think I'll ever forget that day. That was the day I stopped trying. The day I gave up on him. Then it was down the beer and hotdog hole for him. Only for him to end up like this. Dead on the floor with a whole the size of a dinner plate in his abdomen. Michael found a way to cover it up when he moved him to the bed, but I doubt I'll ever forget it. I need to plan a funeral. Oh god, how do I plan a funeral? He did Mom's. They wouldn't let a seven year old plan a funeral.

A hand landed on my shoulder, before running over my back in soft soothing circles. I guess he has been here this whole time. He sighed, bracing both hands on my shoulders, "Eight thousand, eight hundred and twenty two seconds."

"Really?" I coughed out. Michael chuckled behind me, "Wow. So you're comforting me, *and* laughing. I guess that's how I know this is bad."

"Your last parent just died. I don't think you need General Michael of the Almighty Forces of Zion right now."

"Is that your full title?" I shifted, finally looking at him. "It's a little long winded, don't you think?"

"No," He scoffed, "It commands respect. Now, what is the next step after a human dies?" My throat burned as my eyes lowered from his, "I apologize. That was insensitive."

"You're okay. The next step is a funeral. We bury him in the ground. I know where my mom is buried, maybe that funeral home will be able to let me know how exactly I'm supposed to do that." That should be a fun visit. "I have no idea what I'm supposed to do with- Um. With..."

"I understand. I will handle it." He squeezed my shoulder, "Come on. You need to sleep."

He's kidding, right? I can't sleep right now. I need... I don't know what I need. I need a walk. Outside. "Yeah. I'm going to do that." Michael let me go. At least, I think he did. I don't really know if I'm honest. It felt like someone had shoved a handbell in my skull and shook me like a crowded Etch-A-Sketch. I slipped on my tennis shoes, and made my way out front.

The neighborhood was silent except from the ringing that persisted. Mrs. Mitchell was outside of her house getting her mail when I passed. She scowled at me, but that isn't really a new thing. I crashed my bike into her flowerbed when I was ten and she has never forgotten. She's known my family since I was born. Would she come to the funeral? I can't remember if she went to Mom's.

There was no one else wondering around outside as I strolled. Strange for this neighborhood. There's almost always kids outside, or people walking their dogs. Especially that group of teenage girls that's started to hang around every time they see Michael's car in front of the house. He waved to them the other day, I think he nearly gave one of them a heart attack. They were new to the neighborhood; moved in a few years ago. So, I doubt they'll be there.

I'm going to have to make invitations. Oh god and a eulogy. I'm terrible at writing. What am I even going to write? Who am I supposed to be inviting, anyway? It's not like he has friends. And it's been so long since he's left the house. I wouldn't even know how to find out who he was friends with.

"Medusa!" I jumped as two large hands landed on my shoulders. Michael spun me around to glare at me with full force, "*What* are you doing?"

I gestured to the sidewalk, "I'm walking." Is that not obvious? I thought the running shoes, and me going around the block was a good indicator of that.

"You cannot be walking right now."

"Why not? I'm just going around the block. It's okay. The fresh air is calming." I was just clearing my head. Surely he can understand that.

"Then explain to me why you're a quarter mile from your house." What? I can't walk a quarter mile. Though, none of these houses looked familiar. It definitely wasn't the way I took to work. "Medusa, your skin is cold. Even to me. We need to get you home."

"Relax, Michael. It's not cold, that's just you." He's always cold. What does he know?

"*Medusa,*" He growled, "It is twenty degrees outside. That is the lowest it has been for the past *two weeks*. You are coming home. I am not asking." He grabbed my arm, and hauled me to his car. He drove to get me?

"I told you I was going for a walk."

Michael scowled at me, but before he spoke he leaned over to buckle my seat belt. "You still must buckle your seatbelt. You *can* die, Medusa." I sighed, loosening the belt. "And, you did *not* tell me you were leaving. I told you to go to bed, and *you* said that it was a good idea. Then you walked out the door and walked *twenty blocks*!" He glanced at me before refocusing on the road, "Your body temperature is at seventy six degrees. Why does this glass keep doing that?"

"Because when you are angry, you start huffing out frost and freeze everything near you. Glass collects frost just like anything else, Michael." He just sighed at me. Guess he's back to being a quiet brooder.

Chapter Ten

"And now, Elias James Sinclair, husband to Emilia Grace Sinclair, and father to Medusa Sigyn Sinclair, we lay you to rest beside your wife. May the two of you find peace together in our God's heavenly embrace." The preacher continued his never-ending speech over my father's closed casket. Michael stood beside me in a full suit with his hands clasped in front of him. Then there was me, sitting in a ridiculous white lawn chair *surrounded* by empty white lawn chairs.

I sent the invitations. No one came.

"Wait! Wait! Shit! Sorry. Yelling in cemeteries is bad, apparently. You should put a sign up that says that." May made her way across the grass with a few red roses grasped in her hand. "Sorry, I'm late. My manager was being a dick."

"I'm here as well. Terribly sorry about being so late. I meant to get here early, but-"

"You failed." Michael finished for Brian.

My boss slid past Michael to come sit on my other side. May took the seat closest to Michael, not seeming to care about the frost giant standing in front of that chair. Brian pulled three mini packs of tissues out of his pockets and handed them all to me. May pulled one out of the packet and cleaned my cheeks.

"There you go." She rubbed my back, "Alright priest you can continue."

"He's a preacher." Michael corrected, "Please continue."

May and Brian grabbed my hands as the preacher droned on. I rested my head on May's shoulder, and she leaned her head on mine. Brian kept ahold of my other hand for the rest of the speech, and tightened his hand when the casket started it's decent. The preacher waved me up to drop the first flower in the grave. I dropped the red poppies, "I didn't know your favorite, so I went with Mom's."

"May I? No pun intended." I choked out a dry laugh, waving her forward. She dropped on of her flowers in the grave, "I didn't know you, and truthfully, I'm not here for you. I'm here because your daughter is my best friend. I hope, for her sake, that you found Emilia and the biggest bag of *Steamie Dogs* God has ever seen." Then her arms were around me, not caring about the massive wet spot I was making on her shoulder.

"Well, I did meet you, and I don't truly have anything even remotely nice to say about you. That being said, you raised one of the greatest human beings I have ever met, and I thank you for that." He dropped one of the flowers May had brought with her. Apparently she'd brought one for everyone. Even Michael was holding one.

"I do not understand this talking thing you are all doing." He dropped the flower, though. I guess that's something. Plus, he saw a lot of sides of my father, and none of them were decent. Since Michael is so good at curbing his tongue, I doubt he would have anything positive to say. Not that Brian or May did, either, but the thought was there.

"Medusa, is there anything else you want to say?"

"No. Hand me the shovel, please." This was much heavier than I was expecting. Shouldn't shovels be lighter?

"Do you need help lifting that?" Michael came to help even without my reply. "This isn't that heavy."

"So you act the same no matter what's going on then?" Brian interjected. He moved away when we finally got the shovel off the ground, probably for the best. The person most likely to hit him with a shovel *is* Michael.

"He likes to stay consistent." I quipped, finally tipping the dirt out of the shovel. Michael handed it off to the men waiting on the sidelines.

"Want to get a burger?" May asked, tentatively.

"Yes." Michael answered for me. When three pairs of eyes turned to stare at him in shock, he sighed. Did he get replaced with a different angel, and forget to update this angel on his stance against burgers?

"Are you sick? Am I being Punk'd?" I laughed at Brian's comment. It was hoarse and weak, but it was the first real laugh from me since... I can't even remember when.

"I am not sick. Medusa just lost her remaining parent. It is only right she gets her favorite food; even if it is a greasy mess of carbs. I'll even pay for it."

"For the record," May turned to Michael, "As an employee I am obligated to tell you that *Steamie's* steams their burgers so that theirs is actually healthier than the traditional greasy burgers. So technically, it's the healthiest burger Medusa could eat." Michael hummed, not replying, but also not disagreeing with her.

I shook my head, turning to Brian, "Definitely some kind of shapeshifter. Michael is somewhere being held captive, screaming about his hatred of burgers." They laughed. May looped an arm over my shoulders, promising me a super sized basket of fries.

"I'm so glad you think you're funny." Michael snarked, staying behind my small group of friends.

We got to the small parking lot, and May pulled away, "I'll see you at *Steamie's*, okay? Do you want to ride with me?"

"No I'm alright. I'm going to stay with Michael. I'll see you at *Steamie's*. You're meeting us, right Brian?"

"Hell yeah! Love me some *Steamie's*. Meet you there." He waved, heading toward his car.

"Yeah, I parked that way too. See you in a sec."

Michael stayed beside me on the way to his car, ever so silent. I paused when we got to his car, and turned to face him, "Wait. For just a second, I promise." Michael crossed his arms, looking down at me. He didn't seem angry, just as impassive as usual. "Thank you for everything. You've been by my side for the past week and a half, no matter how many times I randomly burst into tears, or stopped moving. You made sure I was eating, and didn't make me any monster foods. And, most importantly, you *came*. No one else was there for the planning, or the eulogy, or the first three hours of that preachers speech about how wonderful of a man my father was. I know May and Brian were there toward the end, and tried to make it, and I appreciate them for that, but I cannot express just how much I truly and honestly have appreciated you during all of this. *Thank you.*" Without Michael, there wouldn't have been a funeral. Every time I spoke to the funeral director, my throat malfunctioned and I couldn't speak. Michael could though. He even helped me with the invitations. "You could've left. I know Yhwh didn't order you to do all of this for me."

"No, he didn't." Michael answered. He had a vein that was becoming more and more prominent each day. I thought it was in reaction to my almost constant crying, but now I'm not so sure. When I said his father's name, his eyes turned to that icy light blue color that screamed murder. "However, my father does not control every aspect of my life, and I wouldn't abandon you during a time like this. I consider myself honorable. Leaving you right now, after the way your father was murdered would make me the exact opposite of an honorable being."

"So you do think he was murdered? Do you know by who, or who would even want to? It's not like he had any enemies. Except for maybe the lady at the cable company when the snow storm stopped him from watching the game."

Michael gave me a scathing look, "You ramble eighty five percent more when you're upset, are you aware of that?" Well I'm getting in the car now. Michael climbed into the drivers seat, reaching over to buckle me in. He keeps doing that. I was going to get it. Once I remembered. "Do I think he was murdered." Michael scoffed under his breath, "Of course I do. He had an enormous hole in his chest."

"Too far." He could kill a moment better than anyone I've ever met.

"I apologize. Would it make you feel better if I promised you *two* burgers?"

I rolled my eyes at him, "That isn't how you apologize. The actual apology was enough."

"That's what Brian does, and you stop being angry with him!"

"No he doesn't. He does that when I'm upset for a reason that doesn't include him. Crying freaks him out. That is completely different from you being callous." I huffed. Exhaustion had settled in days ago. I've been walking through sludge ever since.

Michael just huffed, pulling into a parking spot. May waved us over to the table her and Brian were sat at, "Got you some fries, *and* another surprise is on the way. Probably breaking a speed limit or five."

Brian frowned at her, raising his hands in surrender, "I have no idea what she's talking about."

"That isn't surprising." Michael snarked, taking the seat beside my boss.

I slid into the seat beside May, laying my head back on her shoulder. When the waitress stopped by the table, May rattled off my order along with hers. Michael went ahead and ordered me a second burger along with two for himself. Brian almost had a meltdown at that. Not that I could blame him. Michael was the king of 'I don't eat human food' and then listing the reasons it was a terrible creation. The only person that knows that better than me is Brian. I lost count of how many lectures he's had to endure.

"So are we going to ignore Michael liking burgers now?" Brian asked, once he was sure to scoot his chair away to the giant that was glaring at him. "For the record, he *is* still scary. Just in case you thought that changed."

May laughed at him. Judging from his expression she also called him a bad name when she mouthed something. I couldn't see her mouth from her shoulder, though I wouldn't put it past her. "Medusa, are you going to eat your fries? No one likes cold fries."

"I'm not really hungry." I probably should be. I can't remember the last time I ate. Michael probably has it logged somewhere. He's the one that keeps threatening to force feed me. Honestly I'm surprised he isn't threatening me right now. Being in public shouldn't stop him. I pulled away from May to look at him. He was just staring off into space. "Michael? Are you alright?"

He didn't respond. He just sat there. Motionless. May and I looked behind us, but the wall didn't seem to be doing anything. Even Brian was frowning at him. When he didn't respond to any of us, Brian poked him in the shoulder. Finally, Michael blinked, "I have to go. Medusa, eat something."

"Wait. Wait." I tripped over the leg of my chair, hitting the corner of the table with my hip. Michael caught me, keeping ahold of my arms until I was steady again. "You're leaving me? For how long? Where are you going? What's the matter? What am I supposed to do?"

"Breathe, for starters." Yeah, that's probably good advice. I have no idea what just happened. He got up, and I... Panicked. Maybe that's why he's leaving. I've become too dependent on him. "I need to speak to my father." He pressed his forehead to mine, burying his hand in my hair, "I will be back before you go to bed. I promise."

"Okay." I nodded, going back to my seat, "Okay. Don't tell your dad I said hello, okay? I'd hate to give him the wrong impression."

Michael nodded, "I understand. Take care of Medusa, you two. I am *not* kidding. Even if she's crying, *Brian*."

"Yes, sir." Once Michael was out the door, Brian turned to us, "Why am I in trouble?"

"To be fair," May laughed, "Are you ever not in trouble with him?"

Not usually. Brian scoffed, crossing his arms. They didn't stay crossed for long though. He wouldn't be able to shovel fries in his mouth if his hands were crossed. "I hope you never change Brian." I don't know how I'd react if I lost him too.

"You're about to start crying again. Your eyes are going all red." The fear was palpable in his eyes. It almost made me laugh. May definitely laughed.

"Well that's ridiculous. Medusa would never cry while I'm here." A haughty voice paired with the longest pair of leather pants, leaned on the table. Honey brown eyes met mine, the smuggest smirk I have ever seen with them, "Hey, kitten. Life sucks, wanna talk about it?"

I laughed, pursing my lips at her, "What are you doing here?"

"I came to see one of my favorite girls. May told me about your dad. I'm sorry I couldn't be here in time for the funeral. Z sends her love, she couldn't get away." She grabbed a chair from a nearby table. Kat sat on the chair backwards, with her back facing Brian. The man looked a little perturbed at that, but not more than when she moved the basket of fries away from him. "God, I love *Steamie's* fries."

"Yeah so do the rest of us. That's..." He grabbed the basket of fries from her, putting it back in the middle of the table. "Why it's in the *middle*. It's for sharing. Who are you?"

"I'm that bitch. I assumed that was obvious with the demeanor, and the outfit, and the shoes."

"All I got from that is that you're into women. Not that you're a fry hog."

She gave him a scathing look, "Is he always like this?"

May scoffed, "You're one to talk. You can be the hardest person to get along with. You know that, right?"

Kat gasped dramatically, placing a hand on her heart, "Medusa doesn't think so. Right?"

I just shook my head at her, still smiling. I don't know what it is about her, but for the first time since I walked into my dad's bedroom I could finally feel the fog clearing. May ran her hand over my back soothingly, "You don't have to lie to her. It's okay. Medusa's been through a lot, Kat, don't pester her."

"Here you go!" The waitress unloaded the food onto the table, looking around in confusion at Michael's empty seat. "Did you get a replacement?" She laughed, gesturing to Kat.

"Who was there? Oh, the boyfriend?"

"Michael, yeah. He had to run." I explained, though I'm not sure anyone heard it. I hope he's alright. Speaking to his father isn't exactly the most positive sounding thing in the universe.

"His loss is my gain, right?" Kat winked, skimming her fingers over my hand.

"Are you capable of saying anything that isn't flirting?"

May scoffed at that, "Not when Medusa is involved, apparently." She rolled her eyes at her - our? - friend; not that Kat seemed bothered in the slightest. "She's some kind of lesbian magnet. Same with that *outrageously beautiful* woman that was here the other day. What was her name, anyway?"

"Karma," I supplied, "And we *don't* mention her to 'the boyfriend' deal?" Kat raised her brows at me, "Not like that. He just doesn't like her. It's easier to avoid conflict that way."

"We won't tell him." May promised with the other two nodding in agreement. "That being said, he will find out if you don't eat this food. I don't know how he would know, but I don't doubt that he would."

That's a fair point. I can eat a burger. I love burgers. I swallowed, staring at the burger in my hands. Everyone else dug into their own burger - Kat took one of Michael's. No one seemed to notice my staring contest with my burger... Or the way my hands were shaking. It's just a burger. I can take a bite out of a burger. I just have to move my hands, and my face.

Kat patted my knee when I took my first bite. I guess someone was paying attention. She flashed me an encouraging smile when I caught her eye. I huffed, refocusing. I can do this.

I can't do this. I dropped the half eaten burger back onto the plate. That's just going to have to be enough. My stomach churned as I settled back into my seat. "You did great." Kat soothed, polishing off her own burger. "God I love this place."

"Me too." I just wish I could enjoy it. It's almost like I couldn't *taste* anything I've eaten in the past two weeks.

May rubbed my back, "I'll go pay, and we'll take you home, okay?"

"No need!" The waitress chirped, startling the four of us. "Supermodel man paid before he left."

"How did he..." Brian huffed, "That man isn't human, I swear." Oh, how close he was.

I pushed myself up from the table, twisting my hands in my skirt. Kat slung her arm around my shoulders, "I'd offer you a ride, but something tells me you aren't a fan of motorcycles."

I laughed, resting my head on her shoulder, "I've never been on one, but I'm already queasy so now probably isn't the time to test it." She made a face, squeezing my shoulder. It's going to be a long time before she offers me a ride on that bike again. Michael would probably throw a fit if I got on a motorcycle. He already thinks I'm made out of glass.

"Come on. Michael took your car, so you're with me. Are you coming Brian?"

"Of course. I gotta run by the store, first." So he's never coming. He can't stand having someone else running his store. He complains about the work, but it's all a cover. He loves our little corner of the world.

May turned on the car, but didn't shift gears. I frowned at her, silently asking why she was staring at me like that. Her eyebrows nearly disappeared into her bangs, "Seatbelt?"

"Oh." I shifted, buckling my seat belt.

"You're normally more on top of that." May hummed. She turned like it wasn't a big deal, but I could see the worry in her eyes.

"Sorry. Michael has been doing that so much that I guess it slipped my mind." May smirked at that, but stayed quiet.

Michael's car wasn't in the driveway when we pulled in, but Kat was there; leaning on her bike with her ankles crossed looking like a cover model for some magazine. She smirked, running a hand through her hair before opening my door.

"Nice place you got, but I would love to see a *specific* room." She winked.

I climbed out of the car, smiling at her, "My bed smells like Michael, are you sure that's something you want to endure?" She gagged, pulling away from me. May just looked at us in shock. It was strange to me too, but at least he kept the nightmares away.

The girls followed me into the house. Kat walked over to the oversized recliner, running her hand over the back. Her eyes grew cloudy as she stared at the old fabric. Before I could say anything, she was straightening her spine and settling back into her flirtatious persona. Whatever was going on with her, was gone as quick as it came.

"You alright, Kat?"

"Yup. All good. Got any games? Game nights always cheer people up."

"Ooh! That's a great idea." May cheered, settling onto the floor. "You know, Medusa's never been to a sleep over?"

"I did not." Kat looked downright predatory as she settled onto the floor. I took a seat in between the two, leaning against the couch. "I had my first kiss at a sleepover."

"It took you five minutes." May rolled her eyes.

"*What*?" Kat's attempt at an innocent face was pitiful at best. May didn't fall for it for even a fraction of a second. "Sleepovers are for figuring out your sexuality."

That... Doesn't sound true. "I thought sleep overs were about spending time with your friends, and playing games..."

"That's exactly what they are."

Kat rolled her eyes, "Only if you're boring."

"Or straight." May argued, "Like Medusa and I are."

She frowned, "*Bullshit* on both accounts. I saw the way you talked about the *'outrageously sexy'* friend Medusa brought to *Steamie's*."

"That's not fair." While they bickered, I pulled out the stack of dusty board games from the cabinet by the tv. I can't remember the last time I actually played one of these. "You haven't seen this Karma lady. She can make anyone have gay thoughts. It's the arms, I swear."

"They are really nice arms." I confirmed, settling back into my spot.

"God dammit. Who's this girl? Why is she moving in on my territory?"

I laughed at Kat, "I don't think that's what she's doing." May pulled out a thing of cards from the stack, shuffling them in her hands. Kat was too busy giving me a flat look to comment on the game choice. "I'm serious. She doesn't really seem the type to just jump in bed with someone. Karma can be pretty closed off."

"Good." She sulked, "She can stay that way. The last thing I need on this vacation is someone with '*those* arms' and '*those* abs' wondering around."

"We didn't say anything about abs."

"Anyone who has arms that nice, has abs. I promise."

"She does." I confirmed. Two sets of eyes whipped to my face, "Not like that! She wears a lot of tight tank tops!" All her shirts are tight. Her, Roman, and Michael have that in common. They have to know what they're doing.

Kat huffed, "No wonder you aren't affected by my charms. There's some kind of goddess wondering around."

A knock came at the door before slowly opening. Brian poked his head in the door, "Can I come in?" I waved him in. I really wasn't expecting him to make it back here. He came in holding a filled grocery bag.

Kat perked up at the sight of it, "Alcohol?"

"No. You have met Medusa, haven't you?" He sat down, completing our little circle. He sat the bag down in the center, "Candy. Chocolate bars, gummy worms - sour, because I'm not dumb - and those strawberry things you love. Why are we sitting in a circle?"

"Blackjack. Know how to play?" May asked, sliding the hands between her cards in an awesome and smooth move. One that I could never do.

"Of course I know how to play Blackjack. My parents could've bought college scholarships for your entire graduating class with the money they've spent in Las Vegas." Kat agreed that she knew how to play as well. I suppose now would be a good time to mention that I don't know how to play this game.

"Alright, Medusa. I'm going to run over rules, then we'll play a practice round." Oh I guess she didn't need me to say that. That's good. May went through the rules, which didn't sound so difficult, and started the practice round.

忍

Four hours, and a candy coma later, I was feeling much better. Everyone hugged me on their way out. Kat squeezed me, putting her lips right at my ear, "You're going to be okay, Medusa. You're a lot stronger than you let on." Then she kissed the side of my head, and walked out the door.

Brian made me promise to take the next couple weeks off, but also to call him if I needed him. Meanwhile, he promised me that he wouldn't let Mac and Amita ruin our favorite place.

May promised to come by to spend some time with me so I don't go crazy while I'm banned from working. What kind of boss bans people from working, anyway? She also ordered me to ask her if I want something - *"Anything! I mean it!"* - to eat or snack on.

Once they were gone, I cleaned the kitchen... And the living room... *And* the rest of the house. Michael came back sometime later, pulling the duster out of my hand. "It is time to sleep, Medusa. It's eleven-thirty at night."

"What does it matter?" I sighed, leaning against him. "It's not like I have work tomorrow."

"No?" Oh I don't like that look on his face at all. "Sounds like we have some time to focus on training."

"My father's funeral was today. Can you take it a little easy on me?" He dropped me onto my bed, moving to grab pajamas from my dresser. He threw those at me too. "I guess that's a no." I slipped into my pajamas. I stopped caring about changing in the same room as him a while ago. It's not like he's going to look. "I take it the talk with Yhwh didn't go so well?"

Michael huffed, now dressed in his own pajama pants. He'd gotten them while we were funeral planning in an attempt to cheer me up. It worked a little bit. Who wouldn't laugh at a man like Michael in panda pajama pants. He slipped under the covers beside me, not objecting to me curling into his side. I suppose he's gotten used to my codependency. "It's... Complicated."

"How complicated?"

He ran his hand through my hair, "Even I don't know that yet." Well, that's horribly ominous. "I believe the second Virtue is almost pinpointed."

"Isn't that a good thing?"

"We can only hope." I hope this isn't him trying to make me feel better. He's doing a spectacularly terrible job. Michael's hand tightened on my shoulder, "Don't worry, Medusa. I will keep you safe. I promise."

"Thank you." I take it he isn't going to tell me what he's going to protect me from. Then again, I doubt that's information I want to know. If it's something I need to know, he'll tell me.

"Believe me; it's an honor."

Chapter Eleven

"Dammit!" I flinched as Michael hit the tree closest to him. The tree snapped in half, luckily toppling *away* from me.

I pulled my sleeves down over my hands, and crossed my arms. I thought I had been doing a good job. I still can't grasp the whole fist fighting thing, but I did clear that whole tree of leaves! That's progress. Not enough, apparently, since I've never heard Michael curse.

"I'm sorry, Michael. I'll try harder."

"You're doing a fantastic job, Medusa. You've come so far." He sighed, "That's not what is bothering me." I stayed quiet. Michael was basically word vomiting information. "Your powers are stronger. Which *should* be a good thing, except the only reason they got this strong is because your personal attachment that ties you to your mortal life - and makes you feel inferior - is now gone."

"I don't know what that means."

"Your father dying is what made your powers stronger. Which is *exactly* what they wanted." He cursed again, hitting another tree.

Once the tree - loudly - hit the forest floor, I put my hands on his upper back. The goal was his shoulders, but they're way too high without a stepping stool. He sighed, turning slightly, "Who are you talking about? You know who killed my dad?"

He sighed deeper, "I've had an idea since it happened. There's really only one thing that could leave a clear hole like that in a person. It was Jophiel." He arched a brow at my gasp. "Are you truly that surprised?"

"Why wouldn't I be? Your father had my father killed? For what? I thought he wanted me on his side!"

"My father doesn't think of life the same way others do. Human attachments are frowned upon in Zion. If an angel was to..." His eyes seared into mine, "If an angel was to fraternize with a human, the punishment would be unimaginable. In his mind, he's freeing you."

"Well, in my mind he's a jackass!" I gasped, slapping my hands over my mouth. Michael's brows shot to his hairline. "I know what I said, and I meant it." Michael went to wipe away the tears streaming down my face, but I slapped his hands away. "He wanted me angry. Well, I'm angry."

Wind blew through the trees around us, taking the leaves with it. Leaves of all colors and shapes whirled around the two of us. Michael held a hand over his face, still squinting at me. When I was done, the trees were bare, and we were standing in every kid's dream leaf pile.

"Medusa-"

"Just take us home, please."

Michael brought us back to my bedroom. Once he let me go, I grabbed my things for a shower. I didn't speak to him while I gathered my things, or as I left. When I was out of the shower, Michael was gone from my room. Where did he go? I found him in the kitchen, making lettuce wraps.

"I'm not hungry."

"You will eat at least two, or I will put them in your food chopper and feed them to you as if you were an *infant*."

I scowled back at him, but took a seat at the table. Michael sat down a plate in front of me, and stood over me with his arms folded. I ate while glaring at him until it was gone.

"I'm not angry with you, Michael." I huffed, putting my plate in the sink.

"I didn't think you were, but I am concerned about how this newfound anger will affect your judgment. We can't have you doing anything irrational. We can't locate the other Virtues without my father's help."

"I'm not going to do anything dumb, Michael. I'm not abandoning the other Virtues to this... Whatever he's doing. They don't deserve this." I sat on the couch, leaning my head on Michael once he sat beside me. "I'm not really a *leader*, but I refuse to abandon them in this."

Michael chuckled at that, "I believe you will be a patient and understanding leader of this team-to-be." I was a little too stunned to thank him; not that he seemed to mind. Michael's arm stayed firmly wrapped around me, "And I will be there, so you have someone-"

"That can terrify them and make them behave?" That just got me a 'harrumph' noise, but he didn't deny it.

"I am a warlord, remember?"

"A warlord that really likes brownies." I snorted. I'd used my mom's old recipe when Michael insisted I eat, but I couldn't find anything that tasted good. I only ate two - a personal low for me

-while Michael finished off the rest. Despite him claiming that he threw them away.

"You cannot prove that. And for the millionth time, you are getting off topic." He huffed, "Once we get the location of the next Virtue, we'll go retrieve them, and welcome them into this team we seem to have created." I like him calling us a team. Probably shouldn't share that, though. Michael can't handle too much sappy-ness at one time.

"You're getting emotional. I can *feel* it." That got me to laugh. Michael just grumbled, settling deeper into the couch. "You did a good job today. Maybe a little too much of a good job, considering that trees have leaves for a reason, but still you did well."

"Thank you, Michael. I'm sorry about my outburst."

"No need for an apology. I have had my share of outbursts."

"I would've *never* guessed that."

"Sarcasm is the product of a weak mind." He snarked back, pulling a lock of my hair. I didn't have to look at him to know he was smiling when I yelped. God, he can be mean when he wants to be.

"So is bullying." I stuck my tongue out at him.

"You are a *child*. Do you need a nap?" I scowled back at him, slapping his arm. He guffawed at the attempt, "Magical strength is improving, but your physical strength is still non-existent. We should work on that."

"I thought that was how our team worked? I'm the caring team leader and you're the muscle who doesn't take anyone's crap."

"Oh is that what I am?" I beamed at him, nodding. He sat up, getting close to my face. I stared right back at him, not backing down from whatever kind of challenge this was, "You still need to know how throw a proper punch."

"I think I can agree to that, but no more martial arts. I wasn't made for the superhero life. I'm not a Batkid or whatever they're called."

"I haven't the slightest idea what you're talking about. Come on; break time is over." I groaned letting him pull me up from the couch. Michael took me back outside into the crisp cool air of the evening. I really need him to understand that I can actually get cold. Maybe he should've been Karma's mentor. The cold didn't seem to bother her while she was wearing a tank top at the park the other day. Oh wow, that was much longer ago than a few days now.

"Now here's what you do. Hold you hand like this, put your feet shoulder width apart, and balance your weight evenly. No like this." He moved me to where I was standing the way he wanted me to. "Holding your hand like this will break your thumb. You need to do it like this." He explained why I had to hold my hands a certain way, and how to follow through with my attack. He glared at me when I tried to oppose the thought of me attacking anyone or anything. I'll drop it for now. "Just like that. Good job. Do it again."

He made me repeat the movement several more times with both hands, giving me mini critiques with each repetition. "You can stop now. Excellent job. Next we'll work on different types of punches."

"That doesn't sound so bad. This seems much easier than your other torture methods that you try to pass off as training."

He scoffed, "I can show you torture methods."

"Hard pass." Grumpy old man.

忍

Karma: *'Hey, if I send you something would you be able to make prints of them at your store? Like big canvas prints?'*

I curled around my phone, thankful that Michael had insisted on making breakfast this morning. He gave a long speech about how if I wasn't going to eat a lot then I needed to stuff as much nutrition into what I do eat. I'd prefer to not face that music for as long as possible.

Medusa: *'Yeah! I can do that easily at Whittle Corner. Do you want me to send them to the cabin?'*

Karma: *'Yes, please. How much do I owe you?'*

Medusa: *'How does a burger sound?'*

Karma: *'It's a date.'*

The pictures came through a few moments later. The utterly breathtaking pictures. The first few were of a black skeletal horse with a bright red mane that looked to be entirely made of flames. Black smoke swirled around the horse's hooves, adding to the majestic atmosphere of the photos. The next set was of a similar horse with a white skeletal body and a braided white mane and tail. This horse's bones practically glowed in the pictures. These are *breathtaking*.

Medusa: *'Got them! These are incredible! They should arrive at the cabin by the end of the week.'*

"Medusa." I jumped, clutching my phone to my chest. Michael frowned at my actions, "My father has asked for a meeting with you. Come eat. We need to go."

"Okay. Let me put on real pants." Once he was gone, I went right back to my phone.

Medusa: *'Apparently Yhwh wants to meet with me????? I'm so nervous!!!!!!'*

Medusa: *'Sorry that was a lot of punctuation.'*

Karma: *'Thank you for doing this. I hope everything goes well with that bastard, just remember to stay as calm as you can. Oh, and pretend to buy into his bullshit. He's got an ego, so as long as you stay on the right side of it you should be fine. I gotta go. Mentor gets pissy when I'm late.'*

Yeah, I understand that. Speaking of mentors... I slipped into the first pair of leggings and shirt I found, and darted to the kitchen. Michael had a plate of bacon, eggs, and a small bowl of oatmeal waiting for me on the table.

"I thought you were putting on real pants? Here, you don't have to finish all of it. Do your best." I squinted at him, sliding into my seat. He's being oddly supportive all of the sudden. I stole glances at him as I ate the surprisingly good food. His fists had a slight tremor to them that he seemed to be hiding to the best of his ability. He's upset about this meeting. That's not comforting in the slightest.

I gave up about halfway through. It tasted better than most things I've eaten recently. Maybe my taste buds are coming back. "I'm ready to face the beast."

His lips quirked, "Lets not call him that when we're in Zion." He offered me an arm, and waited

until I was tightly holding on before traveling,
taking us to Zion.

Chapter Twelve

"Patience. Welcome to Zion." Jophiel greeted us with a smile. His eyes, though, were focused on mine and Michael's intertwined arms. I could see the resentment flooding them. "Since this is your first time here, I will go over the rules."

"I have already been here." I straightened my spine, pulling away from Michael. My mentor stayed by my side as I walked past his brother, "And I don't take orders *from you.*" Michael chuckled at that. Jophiel didn't seem quite as amused, though.

"Michael. Medusa. Welcome back." I stayed silent as we approached Yhwh. Karma's warning echoed in my head. Whatever he had claimed 'wasn't that bad' had a direct affect on my friend. One that still meant a lot to her, judging by her reaction. He also ordered Jophiel to kill my Dad. Jophiel wouldn't act on his own like that. He'd be too afraid to face Michael if he got in his way without the proper backup.

"Father," Michael nodded, "You said it was urgent."

"It is. Another Virtue has been located. I'm sending Gabriel to retrieve it. You asked to be made aware when we found it. I'll let you know when it's brought in."

"No." Michael raised a brow when I interrupted whatever he was going to reply with. "*I'm* going to bring in the next Virtue. Michael and whoever Gabriel is, can come with me if they'd like." I crossed my arms, glaring at the man who is credited with creating the planet.

Yhwh raised a brow at me. His golden eyes seared into me. This must be the ego Karma was talking about. It seems I have upset him. Michael placed a firm hand on the small of my back, earning a noise from Jophiel. Jophiel crossed to their father.

"Father, I have a better idea. Gabriel goes to retrieve the next Virtue, Michael returns to his normal duty, and *I* will *correct* Patience."

I scowled, focusing on the annoying angel. Just a *little bit*- Jophiel flew several feet backwards before he came to a stop. He didn't get back up either. Good. My life is much better without him talking. "*Or,*" I refocused on Yhwh, sounding much more confident than I currently felt, "We do this my way."

Yhwh drew a deep breath, his eyes flaring, "I suggest you don't forget who is in charge here." I raised a brow at him, keeping my arms crossed. He doesn't need to know my hands are shaking. "Fine. You will go with Gabriel. Michael you are allowed to return home."

"Thank you, Father, but I am going to travel with Medusa. I find that it's best to not leave her alone." Michael smirked down at me. He doesn't really think I'm some type of loose canon... I hope. But I am glad he spoke up. There's no telling what this Gabriel guy is going to be like. He could be worst than Michael was in the beginning.

"Gabriel is still going to accompany you." Yhwh was still angry, but he rolled his shoulders and moved on. "Your brother will tell you the details of your mission. Go back home and await further instructions."

Yhwh extended his hand toward me, sending the lingering clouds to bolt to us. "Father wait!" Either Michael spoke too late or Yhwh simply wasn't listening, because moments later we were in my living room. My legs immediately gave out, landing me on Michael's arm. "I've got you."

"Thank- Let me go!" Shock flittered across his face as he released me. I darted down the hall to the bathroom, not bothering to close the door. I doubt Michael would follow once he heard these noises.

When I was done heaving, I settled back against the bathtub. Michael handed me a damp washcloth, and flushed the toilet. "I didn't realize you were in here." I rasped, wiping my face. "That feels nice. I need to brush my teeth."

"I second that." I shot him a glare, and let him help me back to my feet. Michael stayed by the door while I cleaned myself up. Once I was done, he slipped his arm under my knees and swept me off my feet.

"Are you carrying me?"

"Yes. Your balance is off. You need rest."

"I'd argue, but I'm super tired."

忍

"Am I in Hell? This is my Hell. You know it's almost Christmas, right? I thought you liked me. I thought we were friends." Brian paced the floor of the break room, pulling on his beard.

I'd told him about my 'vacation' when I first came into the store. That's when the rant started. Then, I made the canvases for Karma, wrapped them securely, sent them to the address she had sent, and deleted any trace of Karma's magical pictures from the systems. After that, I went back to see if Brian had finished his rant, and found him still ranting as if I never left the room to begin with.

"Would you believe me if I said that I'm sorry?" I stepped in his path, effectively making him stop pacing.

"No." He scowled, "No, I wouldn't. You're going on a vacation with your gladiator boyfriend to god knows where, and leaving me here with the rest of my employees that can't make up a fourth of you! No, no. An eighth. They can't make an *eighth* of you! You're abandoning me!" Okay, so he's really upset.

"I'll bring you anything you want back from my trip?" I bit my lip to stop my smile.

Brian raised his brows at me, "You know what I want? My best employee back without a massive diamond on her finger that means she doesn't work anymore."

I rolled my eyes at him. Like I would ever marry Michael. "We aren't getting married. I will be back in a few weeks. I *promise*. You banned me from working for a few weeks anyway, remember?"

"So? You're Medusa! I figured you'd last a week before clocking in while you made Michael glare at me so I couldn't stop you. I didn't think you'd actually take a vacation! Argh! You're lucky I trust you." He huffed, "Have fun on your trip. Don't forget about me."

"I would never." I kissed his cheek, and squeezed him as tight as I could. "You're one of my favorite people."

"You'll have your job waiting for you when you get back. Try to see if you can tan. You're looking a little ghostly." I laughed at that. He knows just as well as I do that this skin is only capable of burning. The chances of me getting a tan without a spray is impossible.

"Thank you." Now time for the next stop.

I made my way down the street to *Steamie's*. May waved at me when I came in, and finished whatever she was talking about with her current table. "Hey! How've you been? I wasn't expecting to see you so soon."

I gave her a tight smile. This is harder than I thought it would be. "Hey, I wanted to say goodbye. Michael and I are taking a little vacation, and I won't be back for a couple of weeks."

Her brows furrowed as her eyes searched my face, "Are you sure that's a good idea?"

"Yeah," I was being totally honest, too. This didn't feel like me running away from dealing with what happened to my father. It felt like I was finally taking the first real step toward my destiny. "Trust me. This is going to be a really good thing for me, and I'll be back before you know it."

"Well," She wrapped me in a tight hug, "I'll have a table waiting for you when you get back. Bring me something cool from wherever your beau takes you."

"I can do that." I promised, giving her another hug. "Tell Kat I'll see her when I get back. Oh, and Zelda. I like her too. Maybe we can have a girl's night."

"Sounds like a plan." She beamed at me, "Maybe you can even bring the fitness model back with you."

"I'll see what I can do." I laughed. The chances of Karma ever joining in on a Girl's Night is incredibly slim, but it wouldn't hurt to ask. Though, I don't know if Telluride could handle Kat and Karma teaming up. Heck, I don't know if *I* can handle the two of them in the same room. "Take care, May. I'll see you soon. If you don't mind, can you stop in and check on Brian? He's not handling this well."

"See you soon, and yeah I can. He's a pretty cool guy. If you end up on a beach, send me a bikini picture. I'll need it if I ever need to Kat to do something." I snorted at that, and did *not* promise to send her one. I could still hear her cackling as I left *Steamie's*. For such a nice person, she can be pretty diabolical.

Now that my friends know Michael wasn't kidnapping me, it's time to head back home. Michael said his brother Gabriel should be there by the time I made it back. I can't say I'm too excited about meeting another angel. Michael was a nightmare, and gave me several bruises when we met, Adakiel was unnerving and almost got me fired, and Jophiel murdered my father *and* got me to curse. In short, angels kind of suck. Michael is better *now,* but we only got this close to a friendship after he made me contemplate throwing myself off the nearest bridge. At least bridge jumping wouldn't hurt as bad as Krav Maga did, and don't even get me started on that other one I can't remember the name of. I'm just glad he settled for basic punching. He can do the rest of the kicking and special stuff.

Epilogue

"Medusa, welcome home. This is my brother Gabriel; he is an Archangel as well." Michael was standing in the living room with a man of a similar height and build, but this man had dark brown hair and warm brown eyes. He smiled at me when I caught his eye. Like and actual *genuine* smile. Is Michael sure he's an angel?

"It is wonderful to meet you, Patience. My brother has informed me that you prefer to be called by your human name, is that correct?" I nodded silently, stuffing my hands into my pockets. Maybe I should just be nice while he is. "Medusa it is then. I am Gabriel, messenger of Yhwh, and the patron of communications."

"Which is why you're here; to help us communicate with the next Virtue. It's nice to meet you, Gabriel." Even if you are a strange angel.

"You as well!" He clapped, making Michael sigh. "Now, time to talk about the next Virtue and where to find her. It was actually your intel Michael that helped us find her. Her name is Jezebel Nacar, and she lives in *Aurora de Numismata*, Italy. We have set up a base to house the three of us while we are there retrieving Chastity."

"Chastity? Is that he Virtue we're going to get?" What is that going to be like? What would the physical embodiment of Chastity be like?

Michael did not look as excited as I felt. In fact he looked even more upset than he did before,

"Stop looking so excited. You're forgetting the fact that Jezebel has seen you."

"That's only if she remembers the dream."

"You remember the dream why wouldn't she?" I settled for sticking my tongue out at him, and heading into the kitchen. "Where are you going? I already packed snacks for the trip."

"Snacks?" Gabriel asked, mimicking his brother's crossed arms.

"Yes." Michael nodded, "Medusa needs to be able to access food at all times. She hardly eats, so when she *is* hungry she needs to have access to food."

"I thought humans were on schedules."

Michael gave him a flat look before gesturing to the isolated bag in my hands, "First lesson, brother; Medusa is on her own schedule since she is team leader. Everyone else is following her schedule. Including us."

I have a feeling laughing would ruin whatever lie he's trying pull off, and it's definitely a lie. Michael has never followed me anywhere. He normally just grabs me and flies us to wherever he deems we need to be.

Gabriel didn't seem to catch on, though, "I will keep that in mind. Are you ready to go then, Medusa?"

"Sure! How are we traveling to Italy anyway?"

A set of firm hands landed on my shoulders. I turned my head, trying to see Michael's face. I shouldn't have done that. He's smiling. Michael smiling *can't* be a good thing. "Probably shouldn't have asked." What does that mean?

Oh my God. The floor disappeared from beneath us, being replaced with clouds. Clouds!

"Michael!" His arm stayed firmly wrapped around my waist as his wings flapped. Gabriel was beside us with all three of my bags in his grasp. His wings were white like his brother's but with a much shorter wingspan. They have the same build shouldn't they need the same size wings?

"Stop squirming. I won't drop you."

"Why are we *doing* this? I like the other way of flying. The one where I don't have to see *the actual flying!*" Well good news, I learned something new about myself. I hate flying.

"Italy is too far for that method, I'm afraid. Just relax." I don't believe him. If we can make it to Heaven, we should be able to make it to Italy. He just likes seeing me panic.

Hours later, we landed in the same meadow from my dream. I planted myself on the ground as soon as he let me go. "Next time, we're taking a plane. At least those have seats. Flying is only for trips shorter than an hour."

"That was shorter than an hour. It was a thirty minute flight, Medusa. Thirty-two minutes specifically." Gabriel unhelpfully added, "Oh. Would you like a snack?"

"Sei tu! Sei tornato!' The woman from my dream knelt beside me. She placed a gentle hand on my forearm, *"Ti senti meglio?"*

"Medusa, you aren't replying to her."

I frowned at Gabriel, "And how do you expect me to do that? I took French in high school, and I don't even remember most of that."

He blinked, "Oh. Why did you not say so sooner?" He poked my forehead with two fingers.

"Miss? Did you find whatever you were looking for?" She's speaking English? No that would be ridiculous. This must be Gabriel's magic. Well, that's useful.

"I did, yes. My name is Medusa."

Surprise washed over her face, "You learned *Italiano* since our last meeting! How wonderful!"

"Yes! Yes, I have. Um..." She remembers! What am I supposed to do now?!

"Excuse me, miss, we are looking for the *Monasterium Quod Patientia*. Do you know where it is?" Gabriel butted in, smiling down at the woman.

"Of course I do." She laughed, "I will show you. Are these men companions of yours?" She glanced nervously at the two towering men behind me.

"Yes, we are." Michael stepped up, excluding a charm I didn't know he possessed. "We are here to explore the Monastery, and see this stunning town."

Jezebel smiled at him, raising to her feet. I suppose I should get up as well, now. "Oh wonderful! The nuns are so kind, and the city is beautiful this time of year!"

Alright. Step one complete, now we just have to get Chastity on our side, convince her we're not crazy, figure out what kind of magic she has, and train her to use that magic. Shouldn't be too hard.

Right?

Author's Note

Thank you for reading Patience, the first book in The Event Horizon: Virtues Series. I hope you enjoyed getting to know these characters as much as I enjoy writing them. Medusa is dear to my heart, and I am so excited to finally share her with the world.

If you wish to see more of these characters, or see some sneak peeks of things to come, you can find me at

jasminejohnsonbooks.com
@sins-virtues on Tumblr
@Jasmine_Johnson_Books on Instagram.
@jasminejohnsonbooks on Facebook

Made in the USA
Columbia, SC
13 March 2020